"Do you object to having me as a boss?"

There was a dangerous sparkle in Tagg's brown eyes as he regarded her steadily.

"I didn't say that. But I understood our relationship was to be administrator and client."

"I wasn't aware we had a relationship," he said, deliberately misunderstanding her. He went on before she could respond. "Anything's better than being beholden to me, right?"

He was disturbingly right, but as he was walking away from her door, she felt she wanted to keep him there. "Tagg . . ." she began, not even sure what she wanted to say.

He paused. "Was there something else?"

"Yes . . . I mean, no. I just . . ." Tongue-tied with confusion, she could only look at him. Surely she couldn't be feeling what she thought she was—this almost forgotten desire to be kissed and to kiss back?

Valerie Parv had a busy and successful career as a journalist and advertising copywriter before she began writing for Harlequin in 1982. She is an enthusiastic member of several Australian writers' organizations. Her many interests include her husband, her cat and the Australian environment. Her love of the land is a distinguishing feature in many of her books for Harlequin. She has recently written a colorful study in a nonfiction book titled *The Changing Face of Australia*. Her home is in New South Wales.

Books by Valerie Parv

Man
Shy
Valerie Parv

Harlequin Books

TORONTO • NEW YORK • LONDON
AMSTERDAM • PARIS • SYDNEY • HAMBURG
STOCKHOLM • ATHENS • TOKYO • MILAN

Original hardcover edition published in 1987
by Mills & Boon Limited

ISBN 0-373-02896-2

Harlequin Romance first edition March 1988

CHAPTER ONE

'I PROPOSE a toast to the happy couple—to Karen and Kevin, a lifetime of happiness.'

Although she raised her glass dutifully, Alita couldn't help wondering how much real happiness lay ahead for her friend, Karen, and her grazier fiancé. She realised her viewpoint was tarnished by her own experience, but so many marriages started full of hope and dreams, only to fall apart as soon as the realities of mortgages and children appeared.

She winced at this thought. Children! She could hardly bear to think about children without feeling that old, familiar ache inside her. Sally's death had nearly destroyed her.

A nudge at her elbow drew her back to the present. 'Drink up, Lee, my love. The champagne isn't all that bad, even if it is domestic.'

At her friend's affectionate use of her nickname, Alita forced a smile. 'The champagne's fine, Karen. I was thinking of other things.'

A frown darkened Karen's pretty features. 'I know exactly what other things. You promised me you would think happy thoughts tonight. It isn't every day that your best friend gets engaged, after all.'

Impulsively, Alita hugged her, being careful not to spill champagne over them both. 'You're a fraud, you know that? You two have been engaged for months now.'

Karen grinned. 'I know, but mother insisted on the formalities.' She looked around at the large, noisy crowd. 'I barely know half of these people. I think she invited most of Orange.'

Alita nodded. 'I got the same impression.'

Karen's worried frown deepened. 'You're not looking for Steve in this crowd, are you? Because he isn't here— I wouldn't invite him, you know that.'

'I know, but I can't help looking for him everywhere I go. Doctor Mather says it's obsessive and I agree, but it's as if he's haunting me.' Tears misted her eyes and she fumbled for a handkerchief. 'I'm sorry, I didn't mean to spoil your party.'

'And you haven't spoiled it,' Karen said impatiently. 'But I wish you'd reconsider about looking after my business for me while I'm on my honeymoon. In a completely new environment, you might stop expecting to find Steve around every corner. It would give you a couple of months' breathing space.'

'You're probably right,' Alita sighed, 'but the very thought of going into a strange business, in a completely strange community, terrifies me.'

'I don't see how you can call it a strange business, running a farm secretarial service. Your diploma is as good as mine, even though you've never put it to use. And Walgett is hardly a strange community. You're country born and bred—you'd get used to the western plains in no time.'

Karen sounded more determined than ever to get Alita to take over the running of the small but healthy business she'd built up, looking after the administration of several properties in the north-west of the state. It was true that Alita was equally qualified to handle the work.

After the two girls had completed their schooling in Sydney, they had both gone to Orange Agricultural College to obtain their diplomas in farm secretarial studies. But whereas Karen had struck out on her own, building up a clientele of farmers who preferred to let someone qualified handle their administrative worries, Lee had returned to Sydney. There she had combined her backgrounds to work for an agricultural machinery supplier. It was there that she had met Steven Perry. He was also country born and living in the city, working as a representative selling tractor parts. Their meeting had seemed to be so fortunate at the time, but later turned out to be an appalling mistake.

Karen snapped her fingers. 'You've gone again!'

Lee blinked. 'I'll think about your offer,' she conceded.

An expression of triumph lit Karen's features. 'Well, that's something, at least. I didn't want to pressure you, but I'm really stuck. There isn't anyone else I can trust to look after my business. Look, I'm expecting my American friends to turn up at any minute. Let me introduce you to someone who might help you to make up your mind.'

She grabbed Alita's arm but Lee resisted the pressure. 'Please, don't worry about me. I'm quite happy where I am, enjoying my drink—which is excellent champagne, by the way—and watching the passing parade.'

Karen looked dubious. 'If you're sure?'

'I'm sure.'

She had spoken bravely, but as soon as Karen disappeared back into the throng Lee let out a heavy breath, like a balloon suddenly deflating. She wasn't happy where she was at all. In truth, she wasn't happy anywhere these days. Maybe she should accept Karen's offer and try running the farm secretarial business. She may as well be unhappy there as here, among so many memories.

At least it would relieve her of the terrifying task of job-hunting. Her parents had made it clear only yesterday that, much as they loved her, she was disrupting their peaceful retired existence and would have to start fending for herself again soon. She could hardly fault them, since they couldn't know the whole sordid story of her marriage. And she had already been back at home for three months. It was time that she picked up the pieces of her life and carried on. She had already considered the alternative and rejected it. No matter how low she felt, Steve simply wasn't worth killing herself over. Doctor Mather, bless her, had helped her to see that.

'You're wearing a mighty unhappy look for such a happy occasion,' said a voice in her ear, startling her.

She looked up—this being a novelty in itself, for she was five feet eight inches tall—into a pair of alert brown eyes under heavy, brooding eyebrows. The man's stare was so disturbingly direct that she dropped her gaze and found herself staring at a narrow, arrogant mouth which tilted up at the corners, etching furrows into sun-browned skin.

'I'm sorry,' she said, pretending not to have heard his comment about her expression.

'Precisely. What I'm curious to know is, sorrowing for what?'

'I didn't say I was sorrowing. I was being polite. I didn't catch what you said.'

He was maddeningly sure of himself. 'Yes you did,

but if you insist, I'll go along. You were deep in some private sorrow which made you look unutterably tragic. I decided to come over and cheer you up, since Karen is too busy to introduce us.'

Now she had it. Judging by the Texan drawl, he was one of Karen's American friends. A group of them, including a long-time penfriend of Karen's, were touring Australia and had stopped off in Orange to visit her. Since Lee didn't want her behaviour to reflect badly on Karen, she forced herself to smile. 'Is that better?'

He appraised her carefully before pronouncing, 'Much better. Now the expression matches the beauty of its owner.'

She felt the colour drain from her face. Compliments reminded her too vividly of Steve's parting threat, 'If I can't have you, no other man shall.' She made herself concentrate on the man beside her, and was even more alarmed. The raffish crinkles around his eyes, and the outdoorsy furrows marking his brow, made him look like a throwback to the screen heroes of the past. He was lean and muscled, with carelessly combed auburn hair threaded with sunstreaks. His very demeanour took it for granted that she wanted to talk to him.

'How many out of ten?' he asked after a few minutes of her silent appraisal.

This time she was genuinely perplexed. 'I'm sorry?'

'Do I rate a ten, or what?'

She looked away. 'I shouldn't be staring. I'm . . .'

He grasped her elbow with implacable firmness. 'Apologise once more for living, and you *will* be sorry.'

The pressure of his long fingers against her arm stirred a feeling of unease in her; he misunderstood it and dropped his hand. 'Hey, I didn't mean to hurt you.

Now I'm the one who's sorry.'

Hastily, she pulled on her veneer of composure, fragile though it was. It was a mental trick Doctor Mather had taught her. 'Like putting on a cloak, imagine it covering you from shoulders to ankles, protecting you,' the doctor had said in her soothing voice. Lee managed a wan smile. 'It's all right. I . . . I've been ill and I'm still not fully recovered yet.'

'Now I really am sorry. Hell, I've been talking to you for five minutes and all we've done is apologise to each other. Isn't that something?'

Considering it was the most direct conversation she'd had with a stranger for months, it *was* something, but he wasn't to know it. And she wasn't about to enlighten him. 'I take it you're here on a visit,' she said from under her mental cloak.

He nodded. 'I don't get much time off, so Karen's engagement party is the perfect excuse for a break.'

So he'd come all the way from America for the party. Lee was impressed. 'Your accent sounds Texan,' she speculated.

He smiled and the Cary Grant eyes were framed in laughter lines which Lee found oddly reassuring. 'Guilty as charged, ma'am. Actually, I was born in Australia but my mother was from San Angelo. I grew up there, but I still think of myself as an Aussie.'

No wonder he reminded her of the cowboys she'd seen on American westerns. 'San Angelo sounds like a frontier town,' she observed.

'Maybe, a hundred years ago. These days it's a city of over sixty thousand people,' he explained. 'But there are still wilderness areas. I spent many vacations camping on the high plains beyond the Pecos River where you'll find some of the finest scenery anywhere.'

In spite of herself, she caught some of his enthusiasm. 'I've never been to America, but I'd love to see it,' she commented. 'Although Australia will always be my home.'

'I know just how you feel,' he agreed. He looked at her with fresh appreciation. 'You know, you're very attractive when you relax. You should do it more often——'

'Would you mind getting me a fresh drink?' she asked, cutting him off.

He shrugged. 'Whatever you say.'

She knew from the odd looks he gave her that she had handled the encounter badly. He couldn't be blamed for wanting to chat—that was what parties were for. If only she looked more like part of the furniture, he wouldn't be so interested in knowing her. But, thanks to Karen's entreaties, she had agreed to wear Karen's silky white sheath which tied across one shoulder. Lee thought it emphasised her too-thin figure but Karen insisted she looked model-like and elegant.

While the Texan moved towards the bar, she glanced around for a way of escape. She didn't want to be here when he returned, expecting a proper introduction.

Karen's parents' house was one of many rambling old homes which had once been on the fringe of the city of Orange, and were now engulfed by new housing estates. But it still boasted a wraparound veranda and several rooms opening on to it. The living-room was one such.

She eased her way through the laughing, chattering groups until she located a pair of french doors which were open to let fresh air circulate. The freedom of the night beckoned.

As she made her way towards the doors, she caught sight of herself in a full-length mirror and she let out an involuntary gasp. She had told Karen she felt haunted but she had no idea she looked so wraithlike and vulnerable.

Her ash-brown hair was short—nunlike, Steve called it derisively—to draw attention away from her looks. Instead, the curling tendrils framed her oval face and accentuated her high cheekbones and hazel eyes which were gold-flecked at the iris in contrast to the pearly whites. They looked large and luminous in her pale face. Feral eyes, Steve called them. He used to say he couldn't take his own eyes off them. But he had, very easily, when something she said or did had annoyed him.

She looked away from the creature in the mirror and gave her attention to her escape route. A glance back over her shoulder warned her that the Texan was making his way back to where he had left her, two glasses held aloft. She dived for the door.

Just as she reached it, a man came through it, his eyes raking the gathering. Instinctively she shrank back behind a large floral arrangement. He hadn't seen her yet but he would in just a moment or two.

'Steve!'

Her lips formed the word unwillingly, and her whole body tensed in protest. He couldn't be here. Karen had promised. Then she realised Karen didn't have to invite Steve. Lee's parents had already intercepted several phone calls from him. They might have felt they were doing her a favour by telling Steve where to find her. If only they knew!

There was only one course open to her. She spun

around and hurried back to the Texan, who was looking for her.

He smiled as she came towards him. 'There you are. I thought you'd run out on me.'

Her answering smile was wooden. 'I thought I saw someone I knew over there.'

'I'm glad you didn't. I was looking forward to a proper introduction.'

Over the Texan's shoulder, she saw Steve moving through the crowd and she lowered her head so she was shielded by the man's bulk. 'I'm Alita Perry,' she said huskily.

'And I'm Tagg Laskin,' he offered. 'I'd shake hands, but it's a little difficult right now.'

He was still holding both drinks and she smiled in spite of herself. There was something reassuring about this man, something so different from Steve. Something less—threatening. And if Steve was in the house then she knew whose company she preferred to stay in! Accepting one of the glasses, she sipped it, thankful for its tranquillising effect. 'And what do you do, Mr Laskin?' she enquired politely, because he was obviously waiting for some response.

'Call me Tagg, please. I'm a sheep farmer, among other things.'

What other things? she wanted to ask, but was too distracted by the thought that any minute now, Steve would find her. She had to do something before that happened. How could she protect herself from him? She'd do *anything* to avoid having to speak to him.

On a sudden impulse, she leaned closer to Tagg. 'Let's not talk about mundane things like work,' she murmured in the most seductive tones she could muster. 'I'd rather know about *you.*'

He looked surprised but interested. 'There isn't much to know. I'm single, if it helps. Had a couple of near-misses but nothing that looked like lasting. Maybe it had something to do with my reputation with the ladies.'

She batted her eyelids a few times. 'A reputation? I wonder if I'm safe being seen talking to you!'

He laughed lightly. 'I didn't say I *earned* the reputation, and in any case, nobody ever came to harm just talking.'

Alita could hardly believe it was this easy. Tagg definitely sounded interested in her. If she could only retain his attention, Steve might pass them by altogether.

'But your likes and dislikes—you must have hobbies,' she prompted in her best Scarlett O'Hara manner.

He looked at her thoughtfully, as if trying to gauge her sincerity. 'I do, as it happens,' he confessed at last. 'But I'm sure you aren't interested in my search for a perennial grass that can be sown after cropping, in hot, dry areas.

If he'd said he was keen on moon walking and making daisy chains, she would have professed enthusiasm. 'Really? It sounds very scientific.'

He took a sip of his drink. 'And very boring. However I do like to water-ski on my property. Ever tried it?'

She shook her head. 'I might be tempted on inland waters, but never where there are sharks.'

'So what does interest you, Alita?'

With every nerve-ending quivering at Steve's near-ness, it was hard to think straight, far less give a sensible answer. 'Dancing and swimming,' she said quickly.

'But not where there are sharks.'

There was a hint of amusement in the tawny eyes as he said this. She had a feeling he meant human sharks, and in this he was correct. She felt as if she was being hunted by one at this very moment. She swallowed hard. 'Can we go somewhere else to talk?' she asked. 'It's very stuffy in here.'

'Just what I was thinking,' he agreed. Taking her glass from her, he set them both down and took her elbow to escort her to the door. Steve was in a far corner, talking to Karen, who looked up and gave a wink as she saw Lee going past. Bless her! She had evidently sized up the situation and was keeping Steve occupied while Lee escaped.

'Don't you want to say goodbye to our hostess?' Tagg asked as she joined him on the front doorstep.

'I'll ring her tomorrow,' she compromised. 'What about you?'

'Since I'm only in town briefly, I'll probably drop by later in the evening—unless I get tied up.'

His comment held a promise of intimacy. He thought they were leaving the party because she wanted to be alone with him! She could hardly blame him, since she had encouraged this conclusion, but how on earth was she to disabuse him? She couldn't tell him she had needed another man to protect her from her ex-husband without explaining the situation, and she wasn't ready to do that yet.

The evening was warm and the velvet sky star-marked. She stood hesitantly on the step, wondering what to do next. Tagg solved the problem for her. 'My rental car's over here,' he suggested.

'Where are we going?' she asked stupidly.

'Wherever you say, ma'am,' he answered gravely.

She knew it was the wrong answer, but she wanted more than anything to be safely home. 'Would you mind driving me home?' she asked.

His expression held even more interest and when they were installed in the front seat of his Bluebird, he rested an arm along the back of the seat, the fingers only inches from her cheek. 'In a hurry?' he asked lazily.

'No—I mean yes,' she stammered, sure now that he would happily spend a lot longer just sitting in the car, although she doubted whether sitting was what he had in mind. She cast him a look of appeal. 'Look, I know I gave you a different impression in there, but I really did want some fresh air.'

His finger brushed the side of her face and she steeled herself not to flinch. 'You gave me the impression that you found me fascinating and wanted to spend some time alone with me,' he said. 'I hope I wasn't wrong.'

What a fool she was to have encouraged him! In her panic-stricken state she had seen it as the one way to avoid Steve. She should have realised that it was better not to start something she wasn't prepared to finish. 'You were right about the first part,' she said carefully.

'So you do find me fascinating?'

She was getting herself in deeper by the minute. 'I meant I found you very interesting to talk to,' she amended.

'Which makes me sound like somebody's grand-father,' he growled. 'I can't be that much older than you. What are you—twenty-three, twenty-four?'

'Twenty-four,' she confirmed.

'And I'm thirty-one, hardly grandpa material.' His eye went to the third finger of her left hand. 'And you're not married. No other commitments?'

She shook her head a little too emphatically. 'Not a chance.'

He dropped his hand on to her shoulder so she was disturbingly aware of the weight of it and the warmth of his fingers against her cool skin. One finger curled under the edge of the fabric, sending a shiver of reaction down her spine. She felt him move imperceptively closer to her. 'Are you sure there isn't a chance—even for me?'

'We've only just met,' she protested. 'It's too early to know how I feel yet.'

'Which means I might have a chance, given a little time,' he said, his voice warming again.

Since he would be back in Texas before she had to deliver on her promise, there was no harm in agreeing. Surprisingly, the thought of his departure gave her a twinge of regret. He was kind and courteous in a way she had forgotten a man could be. His attitude assumed that she wanted him but he was willing to restrain his desires until she made it clear she reciprocated. 'Who knows what might happen—in time?' she said, realising as the words came out that they sounded more coquettish than offhand.

He didn't comment, but instead withdrew his arm and grasped the steering wheel, turning the ignition with his other hand. 'Since my place is too far, it's your place—or your place,' he joked.

Horrified, she clutched at the car door handle. He *had* taken her remark the wrong way! In a torment of indecision, she looked out of the car window in time to see Steve emerging from Karen's house. He stood on the top step, looking around, probably trying to work out where she had gone. If she got out of the car now she would run straight into Steve. Anything was better than that.

In a voice made husky by fear, she gave Tagg her home address, knowing full well that he was likely to read the wrong thing into her acquiescence.

Throughout the short drive, she prayed that her parents would choose tonight to stay home. But her prayers were denied. The house was in darkness when Tagg drove up. 'Mum and Dad must have gone to bed early,' she improvised.

He looked at his watch. 'They must like early nights. More likely they're out for the evening—which gives us the place to ourselves, doesn't it?'

Before she could respond, he walked around to her side of the car and held the door open for her. 'I can manage from here, thanks. And thanks for the lift,' she tried.

'I'll see you to your door,' he said.

There was nothing for it but to let him escort her up the winding pathway to her parents' front door. It was like something out of an old movie, she thought with bleak humour.

As they reached the porch, the shadowy path was illuminated by twin beams from a car's headlights. Without even looking, Lee knew who had driven up. The sound of Steve's car engine was one she had come to dread, and knew as intimately as her own heartbeat. Tagg felt her go rigid. 'What's the matter?'

She had to do something fast, before Steve got out of his car. Acting on impulse, she flung her arms around Tagg's neck and drew his head down. After an initial gasp of surprise, Tagg obligingly sought her mouth and kissed her deeply, sending unbearably sharp sensations all through her.

Then his arm went around her shoulders and he took her key from nerveless fingers, opened the door and led her inside. To an observer, they looked like a courting couple who couldn't wait for the privacy of the house, before falling into each other's embraces. As Tagg closed the door, she heard Steve restart his car and drive off down the street with a screech of tyres.

As soon as the engine noise died away, Lee stepped away from Tagg, regarding him with wide, worried eyes. 'Thanks for bringing me home—goodnight,' she said.

He moved towards her. 'Goodnight? That wasn't the message you gave me a moment ago. What's wrong?'

'Nothing. I changed my mind, that's all.'

'I didn't have you marked for a tease,' he said through taut lips. Only then, she noticed how shallow his breathing had become. She had aroused him when it was the last thing she intended.

'I'm not a tease, honestly. There was someone at the party I needed to avoid. He . . . he followed me home just now and I wanted to give him the impression that we . . .'

'You're worse than I thought,' he swore. 'Using me to make your boyfriend jealous! Why, I ought to turn you over my knee!'

He took a menacing step towards her and she felt her knees weaken. 'D-don't make jokes like that,' she gasped, feeling her face whiten under her make-up.

'I'm not joking, I assure you. I took a liking to you this evening and I was flattered when you asked me to drive you home. Believe it or not, I had no intention of jumping straight into bed with you the second we got

here. I have more respect for women than that. In fact, I
was looking forward to getting to know you better. Well,
now I do. And I'm glad I didn't get any more involved.
The last thing I need in my life is a cheap little flirt who
keeps men on a string. Goodnight, Alita.'

He turned on his heel and walked out, slamming the
front door behind him. Shaking, she raced to it and shot
home the bolt and security chain. Then she made the
rounds of all the windows, checking that they were
secure. Satisfied that she was safe at last, she sank on to
the living-room couch and gave vent to the tears which
had been building up all evening.

They were wrong, all of them. Karen, her doctor, her
parents, all of whom said she could live a normal life
again if she tried. Well, she had tried tonight, and look
where it got her! The first decent man she'd met in years
believed she was a teasing bitch, and Steve had found
her again.

This last sent tremors of apprehension through her
body. How long would he be fooled into believing that
she was under the protection of another man? Knowing
Steve, he would ask around and soon find out that what
he had seen was a brief encounter. She laughed hollowly.
They didn't come much briefer. Well, at least Mr Tagg
Laskin would be on his way back to America soon, with
not even a backward thought about her.

If only she could put him out of her mind so easily.
She knew it was just because he had been kind and
decent towards her, that he lingered so in her mind.

All the same, that night her dreams were haunted by a
lean, muscular cowboy who rode towards her. The
dream faded as he reached to hook her into his saddle.

By morning, she knew what she was going to do.

'Are you sure you want to go through with it?' Karen asked her over coffee when they met in town a short time later.

'Positive. As long as I'm among familiar things and people, I'll always be haunted by the past. I have to get away and start again. I think you're right. Looking after your business is just what I need.'

Karen bit her lip. 'It will be a relief to know my clients are in such good hands. I was almost thinking of postponing my honeymoon.'

'That settles it,' Lee said firmly. 'But will they consider me "good hands"?'

'They will once I tell them your background and qualifications,' Karen assured her. 'There's really only the boss of Mundoo Run to consider.'

Mundoo Run was the property on which Karen's business was based. She travelled to the other properties as she needed to. 'Is there any chance they won't accept me?'

Karen shook her head. 'Not really. I rent my cottage on the property and you'll have the use of it. It's not as if you're applying for a job. They don't have to approve you as they would an employee. It's only that, living so closely with the family, it's better if you get along well.'

'What happens if we don't?' Lee asked worriedly.

'No problem. I could arrange for you to work out of one of the other properties, or in Walgett itself. I was thinking of doing that when I met Kevin.'

Lee's eyebrows flickered upwards. 'Weren't you happy at Mundoo?'

'Of course. They have all the amenities of a small town. But it does get lonely, especially for a single woman. Most of the other women have children to keep them company.'

For Lee, that decided matters. A solitary existence was what she craved more than anything right now. 'When do I start?' she said, smiling.

With a light heart, she listened as Karen outlined the work and living arrangements at Mundoo, and explained how to get there. 'Mr di Falco, the station manager, will probably meet you and take you out to Mundoo,' she said. 'And I'll be waiting to show you the ropes.'

'You'll be living nearby after you're married, won't you?'

'Sure. We're honeymooning in Fiji and coming to live on Kevin's share of his father's land afterwards.'

'Won't your mother mind? I'm sure she wants you to be married here.'

'She does, but I'm prepared to elope if she insists on too much fuss and she knows I mean it.' Karen squeezed her friend's hand. 'I'm so glad you're doing this—for both our sakes.'

For the first time in months, Lee was equally sure she was doing the right thing. The lonely life of a western plains sheep station sounded like heaven right now, provided she could convince Karen's clients to accept her. Especially the boss of Mundoo Run, who sounded as if he might be difficult to please.

It was only when she was back in her own room, going over her wardrobe and deciding what to take, that she remembered she hadn't asked Karen who owned Mundoo. She was about to pick up the phone when she changed her mind. Karen had enough to do with her wedding plans, without nursemaiding her friend.

Besides, what did it matter? From what Karen had said, he must be a family man with children so he must be reasonable. And Lee would be living in her own cottage on the property, so they only had to be civil to each other in business hours.

Before they parted, Karen had promised to spend some time briefing Lee on the business. She could find out about the owner of Mundoo then.

Other than that, all she had to do was work hard and convince the boss and his neighbours that she was as much an asset as Karen had been. What could possibly go wrong?

CHAPTER TWO

THE miles between Orange and the railhead at Dubbo swept past the train window in a blur. They stopped now and then, but Alita was barely aware of it. It was fortunate that she had to leave the train at Dubbo and continue by coach to Walgett, or she might have let herself be carried on indefinitely.

Even with the changes, the journey took only a half-day. She wished it was longer, but this was precisely the kind of apathy Doctor Mather had warned her against indulging.

'Force yourself to do things even when you don't feel like it,' she had advised Lee. 'The willingness will follow the effort, not the other way round.'

The doctor had been guardedly pleased when Alita announced her plans. 'Well, you're as ready as you'll ever be,' she said. 'Now it's time for you to try your wings.'

If only her wings didn't feel so rusty and unready!

After reaching her decision, she had spent a week with Karen discussing the needs of the various clients. Now she was looking forward to meeting them all in person. Some she would work for on a weekly basis, others only once a month.

Only at Mundoo Run was she totally responsible for the administration of the property, reporting to the manager, Ray di Falco.

In her handbag was a letter from him written on Mundoo stationery and welcoming Alita to the 'family' of staff and retainers who peopled the station.

'What is Ray di Falco like?' she asked Karen after she received the letter.

Karen grinned. 'Quite a charmer. Fancies himself as a ladies' man but he's harmless, actually. His wife, Cheryl, sees to it. The one you have to watch out for is Craig di Falco.'

Lee felt a shiver of apprehension. 'Why? Is he a ladies' man, too?'

'I'll say! He's got hands everywhere, so you'll spend a lot of the time fighting him off.'

Lee's pale brow creased into a frown. 'You didn't tell me there was a wolf at Mundoo. Doesn't he have any work to do?'

Seeing that her joke was backfiring, Karen relented. 'Hardly. He's all of four years old.'

Worry gave way to relieved laughter. 'Karen, you're impossible!' Lee exploded. 'I think I'll be able to handle Craig.'

Karen's smile widened. 'That's what they all say.'

Karen painted a picture of a community where neighbour helped neighbour and everyone was closely knit, making Lee feel more and more glad she had taken on the job. Granted, it was only for a couple of months, while Karen settled into married life, but a lot could change in that time. Maybe the job would lead to a permanent position in the western plains district. Steve wouldn't think to look for her there.

She'd seen no signs of him since the night of Karen's engagement party a month ago. Karen was convinced he'd gone back to Sydney. All the same, Lee took the precaution of shopping at unusual times and staying out of sight as much as possible. She also let her parents answer the phone, having finally impressed upon them that she didn't want a reconciliation.

This still worried them, but less so since she told them about her job. They made it clear they still believed marriage was 'till death us do part' but the prospect of having their youngest daughter off their hands again made them much more tolerant.

It wasn't that they didn't love her. She knew they did. But she was an enigma. Grace, her eldest sister, had married at nineteen and straight away set about giving them the grandchildren they adored. Even the middle sister, Kerry, behaved predictably, going straight from school into nursing training. She was now engaged to a doctor in the Flying Doctor Service and planned to work alongside him in the Outback.

Only Lee was an oddity, marrying impetuously against their advice, and now divorced. That Steve had pestered her parents about her whereabouts only proved how much he still loved her, in their eyes. They were tremendously understanding about Sally, but obviously believed the best thing she could do was to have another baby by Steve. Lee, however, though she would never have wished it, had been set free from Steve's clutches by the tragedy of their daughter's death, something her parents would never know. Lee could sense their puzzlement when they looked at her but even now, she couldn't bring herself to tell them the whole story. It was too demeaning. She could hardly believe she had put up with it for three years.

But she was free now, if the hunted existence she endured could be called freedom.

Unconsciously, she squared her shoulders. She *was* free, and she intended to make the most of her time in Walgett to forge a new life for herself.

Gradually, the black soil plains of the north-west, rich

in sheep, cattle and grain, gave way to the small but modern commercial centre of Walgett—her destination. With the other handful of passengers, Lee stood up and stretched, then reached for her hand luggage stowed in the overhead rack.

By the time she got out, the driver had already opened the side of the coach. He lifted out a motley assortment of suitcases and packages including Lee's bulging suitcase. Most of her possessions were still at her parents' home. She intended to send for them as soon as she found a more permanent assignment.

Her luggage retrieved, she looked around curiously at the group of people meeting the coach. Which one was Ray di Falco? Karen had given her a thumbnail description of a stocky, bronzed countryman with sun-darkened skin and bleached white hair under a wide-brimmed hat. No one in the group seemed to match the description.

'Well, fancy meeting you here!' drawled a voice nearby and she tensed. It couldn't be!

But it was. She whirled round to find the Texan, Tagg Laskin, standing behind her. This time he was dressed in a red checked shirt and dust-streaked blue jeans tucked into leather cowboy boots. 'Hello, Mr Laskin,' she said uncertainly, wondering what he could be doing here, of all places. Maybe he and Karen had mutual friends in the area.

In that case, maybe he could help her. 'Would you happen to know a Ray di Falco?' she asked.

She was unprepared for his groan of dismay. 'Good lord—you can't be Lee Coulthard, can you?'

'Lee's my nickname, and Coulthard is my single name.'

He frowned. 'Single name? In Sydney, when I asked

if you were married, you said no. "Not a chance" was the way you put it.'

'Not married doesn't mean never married,' she retorted. She was damned if she was going to explain herself to him and her expression said so.

He shrugged and reached for her suitcase. 'You'd better come with me.'

Her eyes widened. She may have given him the wrong impression at Karen's party, but she wasn't going anywhere with him. 'Just a minute, where are you taking my things?'

He sighed, 'You're waiting for Ray di Falco, right?'

'Well, yes, but . . .'

'And he was to take you to Mundoo Run, right?'

'Yes, that's right. Do you know it?'

'I ought to. I own it.'

If there had been a seat handy, she would have collapsed on to it. 'You own Mundoo Run?' she repeated blankly.

'I told you I was a sheep farmer,' he reminded her.

She shook her head in bewilderment. 'I know. I thought you meant in America, not here.'

He raked a hand through his thatch of sun-streaked hair. 'I don't recall we had time to get down to details. You were too busy trying to make your boyfriend jealous.' He fixed her with a hard, unforgiving stare. 'Evidently your little charade didn't succeed in bringing him to heel or you wouldn't be here.'

It was out before she could stop herself. 'If I'd known who Karen's "boss" was, I wouldn't have come.'

'If I'd known who she was sending, I wouldn't have permitted it,' he rejoined with equal candour.

It seemed he was as much a victim of misunderstanding as she was. 'Didn't she tell you who was taking her place?'

'She told me it was a girl called Lee Coulthard. How was I to know you are also Alita Perry? What other aliases do you use, by the way, just so I can be prepared?'

He made her sound almost like a criminal for having more than one variation on her name. Why, she was willing to bet that Tagg wasn't his full name, either! 'I told you, Lee is a short form of Alita, and for some reason, she gave you my single name,' she said primly.

He folded his arms across his broad chest. 'Now why would she do that, I wonder?'

Probably because Alita had been foolish enough to tell Karen about her encounter with the Texan. No wonder Karen had avoided mentioning her boss's name after that, making the point that she worked with the manager. Lee could hardly wait to get hold of Karen and tell her what she thought of such subterfuge.

'It seems there's been more than one misunderstanding,' she told Tagg. 'It might be best if I returned to Orange on the next coach.'

To her surprise he shook his head. 'Personally, it would suit me just fine, but under the circumstances, I can't allow it.'

His presumption that he could dictate what she did made her bristle but she held her temper with an effort. 'Just what circumstances are you talking about?'

He regarded her strangely. 'You mean you really don't know?'

'Obviously not.' What bombshell was he preparing for her?

'Karen and Kevin Vaughan eloped two days ago.'

She stared at him. 'They *what*?'

'Exactly my reaction. I gather she didn't let you in on

their plans, either.'

'She did threaten to elope if her mother pressured her into a fancy wedding—but I had no idea she really meant it.'

'Apparently she did. The first I knew of it was when I found a note in her office. She left one for you, too, by the way. And some instructions concerning the business on her computer.'

Gradually she took in what he was saying. Karen wouldn't be at Mundoo to help her settle into the strange environment. She hadn't realised how much she had been counting on her friend to help her get through the ordeal. Now she was on her own and worse, she had to contend with a man she had already provoked into disliking her.

'How long before we reach Mundoo?' she asked as he stored her luggage in his four-wheel-drive Landcruiser, his expression stony.

'It's a two-hour drive from town. But we won't get there till after lunch tomorrow.'

'You just said two hours? How can it take us until tomorrow?'

He gave a long-suffering sigh. 'Because we aren't going straight back there today. I'm waiting for a new drive shaft for a solar pump and it won't be ready until the morning. I decided to meet you off the coach, and kill two birds with one stone.'

He looked as if she was one 'bird' he would cheerfully like to finish off, she thought grimly. The prospect of spending a night in the town with him further unnerved her. 'Where will we stay?' she asked.

'I've booked rooms for us at the Safari Hotel in Wee Waa Street. It isn't fancy but it's clean and comfortable.'

At least he had said rooms, plural, she thought with

relief. Since he already believed her morals were suspect, she had half-thought he might expect her to share a room with him. The very idea brought a rush of colour to her cheeks. She pressed the backs of her hands to her face to cool her skin.

He saw her confusion and smiled cynically. 'Don't look so anxious. I wasn't planning to take you up on the offer you made at Karen's place, if that's what's on your mind.'

'I told you, you jumped to the wrong conclusion that night,' she said. 'But since you insist on thinking badly of me, I can't do much about it.'

'Too right,' he said, sounding very Australian for a moment, despite the Texan drawl. 'I usually prefer to make up my own mind about people.'

'And you've already made up your mind about me,' she retorted.

He lifted a quizzical eyebrow. 'Can you blame me?'

Before she could answer, he jumped into the driver's seat, leaving her to climb into the passenger seat alone.

In awkward silence they drove to the hotel which was, as Tagg had warned, a typical country pub with accommodation for travellers on the upper floors. From the sound of laughter emanating from the Miners' Bar as they were shown upstairs to their rooms, the Safari was a well patronised hotel.

The sound gave Lee a feeling of security. As least she wasn't alone with Tagg Laskin.

Her room contained a quaint mixture of old and new furnishings. A brass and porcelain bedstead was the centrepiece and a traditional porcelain water jug stood on a marble-topped stand. In contrast was a television set in one corner, and the puffy continental quilt thrown over the snow-white bed linen.

There was no connecting door between their rooms, she noticed thankfully. The only time they would have to see each other was when they used the communal bathroom a few doors down the corridor. And it was only for one night, she reminded herself. Tomorrow she would be installed in her own cottage at Mundoo Run where her contacts with Tagg Laskin would be few and far between.

She didn't for a minute expect that he would want to have dinner with her, so it was a surprise when he knocked on her bedroom door.

She opened it minimally. He was dressed in a white chambray jacket over rust-coloured drill slacks, the front pleats emphasising his overwhelming masculinity. The top buttons of his white shirt were open, affording her a glimpse of tanned skin and curling chest hair. She drew a shuddering breath, wishing the sight of him didn't play such havoc with her senses. It was so long since she had felt this way about any man, and it was rather overwhelming. 'Yes?'

'I thought you'd be changed by now.'

'Changed? What for?'

'It's after seven, so I thought we'd go out for something to eat. You do eat dinner, don't you?'

She had been so preoccupied with her thoughts that she had forgotten it was lunchtime since she'd last eaten, and then only a sandwich before boarding her train 'I . . . I'm not very hungry,' she denied.

'Well, I am, and I don't enjoy eating alone. Get your things.'

She was tempted to tell him she wasn't coming, but that would be doing what her mother called 'cutting off her nose to spite her face'. She *was* hungry, and since she didn't know her way round the town, she might not get any dinner if she didn't go out with Tagg. 'Give me ten minutes,' she said.

'Make it five,' he responded brusquely. 'I'll wait here.'

The very thought of him standing impatiently outside made her hurry through changing her clothes. In a little over five minutes she emerged, wearing a black crêpe de Chine dinner dress with criss-cross cut-outs at the bodice. It was remarkably demure in contrast to the evening dress she'd borrowed from Karen for the party.

Tagg eyed her speculatively when she joined him. He was probably wondering which dress represented the 'real' Alita, she thought.

'I wasn't sure what sort of place we'd be going to, so I hope this is all right,' she said as she locked her room behind them.

'Fishing for compliments?'

She felt the hated colour suffuse her cheeks. 'No, I wasn't. I just want to do the right thing.'

She tried not to resist as he grasped her arm and escorted her downstairs to the street. Since she had no idea where they were going, she could only follow where he led, wondering where he was taking her so purposefully.

The restaurant turned out to be a restored blacksmith's shop called, appropriately, Smithy's. Framed by a hedge of bamboo, the shingle-roofed house was welcoming and cheerful.

Inside, old tapestries hung from the walls and wooden panelling created shelves for ornaments. An old pot-bellied stove formed a focal point, framed by antique tables made of oak. Most of the tables were occupied.

Although there was no sign of the building's former purpose to be seen inside, the antique furniture and slate flooring made Alita fancy she could almost hear the anvils pealing. She looked around appreciatively.

'I thought you'd like this place,' Tagg said when they were settled at a secluded corner table.

She couldn't resist the taunt. 'In spite of my dubious morals?'

'In spite of my unfortunate first impression of you,' he corrected.

Unaccountably, her spirits rose. Was he prepared to give her the benefit of the doubt, then? She hoped so, for the more she saw of the indomitable Tagg Laskin, the more she wanted them to get along. Since it was the first time in ages she had wanted a man to be friends with her, it was progress indeed.

Tagg was apparently a regular visitor to the restaurant, so she let him order for them both. While he discussed their choices with the waiter, she studied him with interest. She could hardly believe she was actually sitting in a restaurant, about to have dinner with a strange man. Not long ago, the idea would have filled her with trepidation. Even now, her heart was beating uncomfortably fast and her palms were moist, but she had conquered the urge to run from the room, which was something.

She was aware of nodding agreement but didn't really hear what Tagg asked her. It turned out he was seeking her agreement to his choice of dishes, which was faultless.

They started with oysters in a light-as-air pastry with a herbed champagne sauce. This was followed by crown roast of lamb with mint sauce, with a frothy chocolate cheesecake for dessert. Tagg had ordered a robust burgundy wine to accompany their main course, and a half-bottle of Sauterne with dessert, so she felt quite light-headed by the time the meal ended.

'At least you aren't one of those picky females who won't eat a bite for fear of spoiling their figures,' he commented as she finished her cheesecake.

'I'm lucky to have a very fast metabolism,' she said. 'I burn food up as fast as I eat it.' Added to which, she hadn't been eating as well as she should lately, and had lost even more weight, she acknowledged to herself. She had surprised herself with the amount she had eaten tonight.

Tagg sat back and sipped the port he had ordered with their coffee. 'Now the important business is over, how about explaining to me why Karen gave me your single name?'

She didn't want to speculate about Karen's motives until they'd had a chance to talk, so she said. 'I don't really know. I'm not married, as I told you . . . before.' She stumbled over the last part, not wanting to spoil their evening by reminding him of that night. She lowered her head.

'But there must have been a Mr Perry once,' he probed.

'There was, we're divorced.'

Although her tone made it clear that she didn't wish to discuss it, he leaned forward, resting his weight on muscular forearms. 'He ran out on you?' he speculated.

Pride stung her into responding. 'No, I divorced him.'

He nodded. 'Got tired of the restrictions, huh? Decided you were too young to be tied down?'

Anger set her eyes blazing. 'It was nothing of the sort. What happened is nobody's business but mine.'

She knew he was putting two and two together, or at least the two and two he thought he had. Her behaviour at Karen's party had marked her as a good-time girl in his eyes, so he assumed it was the reason for her failed marriage.

For a moment, she was tempted to tell him something of the truth but she couldn't force the words out. Why she should want him to know, she wasn't sure. Only Karen and Marie Mather knew the whole story: Karen because she had stumbled on it on a surprise visit one day, and Marie because Lee needed her professional help and advice.

She became aware that Tagg was studying her thoughtfully. 'I'm surprised your husband agreed to let you go.'

Her head jerked up. 'Why do you say that?'

'Because you're a lovely woman with, I suspect, all sorts of hidden depths. If you were my wife, I wouldn't give you up without a fight.'

'If you were my wife . . .' The caressing way he said it brought a lump to Lee's throat. What would marriage to Tagg be like? Would he turn out to be loving and gentle, or a monster as Steve had done?

This conversation was becoming too personal. 'What did Karen say in her note?' she asked him.

He accepted the change of subject with good grace. 'She apologised for leaving us all in the lurch but said her mother hadn't left her a choice. Since she didn't want her wedding turned into a three-ring circus, they had decided to get married quietly in a civil ceremony, and go straight off on their honeymoon in Fiji. Karen's hoping by the time they get back, the fuss will have died down.'

Lee chuckled. 'If I know Karen's mother, it will take much more than a couple of months to get over this.'

'I take it she's a bit of a dragon.'

'And then some! Olive Ritchie is on practically every

women's committee in Orange. I suspect she's the reason that Karen went off to become a farm secretary.'

'Which explains Karen's choice of career, but not yours,' he noted gently.

Was he assessing her suitability for the task at Mundoo Run? she wondered with a brief surge of panic. 'I have the same qualifications as Karen,' she said quickly. 'I just wanted to try my wings in the city before I settled down.'

'But something went wrong with your plans?'

'Yes. Look, if you're worried about whether or not I can handle the work ...'

'That wasn't my point at all,' he interrupted. 'I'm still curious about you, Alita Coulthard Perry. Which is it to be, by the way?'

'I don't know,' she sighed. 'I suppose Karen gave you my single name because she didn't expect me to go on using my married name.'

He eyed her curiously, 'And yet you do. You gave your name as Alita Perry at Karen's engagement party. Could it be that you still haven't severed your ties with your old life, even though you're legally free?'

He had touched a nerve. When she walked out of the court-house a single woman, she had intended to revert to her maiden name, hating any reminders of her life with Steve.

Yet she *had* given Tagg her married name out of habit—or some other motivation. 'What's in a name?' she asked lightly, trying to shrug the question off as unimportant.

'Plenty,' he said seriously. 'I had a fight on my hands to grow up as a Laskin. My mother's family wanted me to take their name, Burnett.'

He had switched the conversation to himself to

alleviate her obvious distress, and she was grateful. 'What happened?' Lee asked, thankful for the respite.

Tagg took a long sip of his coffee before answering, perhaps weighing up how much he wanted to tell her, a virtual stranger. To her surprise, he went ahead.

'My father, Grant Laskin, went to Texas to study sheep-breeding in San Angelo. In a story-book romance, he fell in love with the rancher's daughter, Dorie Burnett. He didn't think there was any future for them, but she had made up her mind to marry him and she was used to getting her own way.

'I didn't find this out until after my mother died, but she told my father she was pregnant, so he had no choice but to marry her. Not surprisingly, the pregnancy turned out to be a phantom one, although she really did become pregnant later on, after they came back to Australia to live.'

'So that's how you came to be born here?'

'Right. But the novelty eventually wore off and Dorie wanted to go home to Texas—with me. I fought tooth and nail for the right to be raised here with my Dad, but she was given custody and we went back to the States.'

So Tagg did have his private sorrows! Her heart went out to the little boy he was then, torn between two parents and two countries. 'How old were you when you left?'

'Ten. Not a good age to uproot a boy, but I wasn't given a choice. Don't get me wrong, I had the best life that money and power can provide. The Burnetts were not without influence in their area.'

'But it wasn't where you wanted to be?'

'No, it wasn't. I was allowed to spend some of my vacations here, so I kept my ties with Mundoo and with this country. Dorie was all set for me to take over the running of the Burnett ranch from my grandfather, but my heart wasn't in it. Besides, there were plenty of cousins who could do that and I was the last of the Laskins. I had to return in the end, when Dad was killed by lightning when he was out mending fences in a thunderstorm.'

Without thinking, she rested a hand lightly on Tagg's forearm. 'I'm so sorry,' she breathed. 'You hear about tug-of-love children in the newspapers but it must be a heart-breaking experience.'

He looked down at her fingers, splayed across his brown skin. Then he rested his own hand on top and she could feel the searing heat of his touch. 'It's in the past now,' he said dismissively. '*Che sarà sarà*, as they say.'

Although he said it lightly, she had a feeling that the wounds of his boyhood experiences went deep, as deep as her own emotional scars. But, like her, he had papered them over so the outside world couldn't see them. Why he had chosen her to share his confidence, she wasn't sure. Was it because he sensed a kindred spirit? Or was it because he thought so little of her that it was like telling your life history to a stranger?

'Enough about me,' he said brusquely, as if already regretting that he had told her so much. 'I trust Karen has briefed you on what's expected of you at Mundoo?'

'She gave me a very good idea, luckily. I was hoping she'd be there to show me the ropes, but since she won't, I'll have to do the best I can.'

'I just hope it's going to be good enough. Mundoo is a vast operation,' he said drily.

The change from confidante to interviewing boss brought her to her senses with a jolt. She would do well to remember their relative positions if she was to keep Karen's business intact until she returned.

Slowly, she withdrew her hand from his arm and cradled it in her lap. 'I'm aware of the scope of your operation, Mr Laskin,' she said coolly. 'I also understood from Karen that while you might be the boss of Mundoo, you aren't my boss, as such.'

There was a dangerous sparkle in the brown eyes as he regarded her steadily. 'Do you object to having me for a boss?'

'I didn't say that. But I understood our relationship was to be administrator and client.'

'I wasn't aware we had a relationship,' he said, deliberately misunderstanding her. Before she could respond, he snapped his fingers for their bill. When she reached for her purse, he forestalled her. 'I'll get this, since I invited you out.'

'I'd really rather pay my own way,' she insisted.

'Anything's better than being beholden to me, right?'

He was disturbingly right, and Alita was silent as they headed slowly back to the hotel, regretting her snappiness. Tagg also said nothing, and she wondered what he was thinking.

He left her at her door and was walking towards his own room when she felt an insane urge to keep him near her just a little longer. 'Tagg ...' she began, not even sure what she wanted to say.

He paused, his hand grasping his doorknob. The silence between them became electric. Slowly, he came back to her. 'Was there something else?'

'Yes ... I mean, no ... I just ...' Tongue-tied, she could only look at him, feeling tension vibrate through her.

She was confused. Surely she couldn't be feeling what she thought she was—this almost forgotten desire to be kissed and to kiss back?

As if he sensed what was in her mind, Tagg stood looking down at her, framed in the doorway. Suddenly, he cupped his hand into the small of her back and drew her against him, bending his head.

It happened so swiftly that she had no time to tense herself, and the onslaught against her senses was devastating. She was aware of the warm pressure of his flesh against hers, and the musk scent of his aftershave lotion. She tasted the port he'd drunk after dinner, and the faintest tang of spices from their meal, plus an indefinable maleness which blended the whole into a heady pot-pourri. Her nose and mouth were filled with him, tastes and scents she'd denied herself for months.

The pressure against the small of her back increased until she could feel his powerful body outlined against hers. Its stirring warned her that this was getting out of hand and instinctively, she tried to pull away.

'Not getting cold feet again, Alita?' he murmured.

Oh God, she'd done it again, letting him think she wanted him as much as he desired her. Was her body trying to tell her something her head wouldn't acknowledge?

The old panic returned and she struggled. 'Please, let me go.'

He released her and looked at her coldly. 'What's the matter with you, Alita? You respond as if you're panting for it, then the minute things get serious, you turn off. Is this some kind of game with you?'

Her eyes misted. 'No, it isn't that.'

'Then what the hell is it?'

How could she tell him of the unpleasant associations and memories a man's touch aroused in her? He would be understanding, certain that he could help her overcome it—like the last two half-hearted dates she'd tried. But nothing could overcome her unwillingness to become involved with a man again, to put herself at risk. She had Steve to thank for that. 'I'm sorry,' was all she could say.

'You will be,' he ground out. 'You have to learn that you can't play with a man's emotions as you've done with me.'

'What are you going to do?' she asked fearfully.

'It gets mightly lonely for a woman at Mundoo. Sooner or later you'll think of this night and maybe wish we could be closer, but you'll have to beg me before I touch you again. We'll see how you like a taste of your own medicine.'

Without looking back, he strode away, and soon afterwards his door slammed shut with jarring finality.

CHAPTER THREE

AFTER a sleepless night, Lee wasn't surprised to arrive in the hotel dining-room ahead of Tagg. She knew he was awake from the sounds she heard emanating from his room, but he didn't emerge until she had used the communal bathroom, returned to her room and dressed, and found her way downstairs.

He came into the dining-room only seconds behind her, his sun-streaked hair glistening from his shower. In spite of her decision last night, she felt a twinge of regret that she wouldn't be seeing him again after today.

'Good morning, sleep well?' he stated, rather than asked, his tone impersonally polite.

'Yes, thank you. How about you?'

'Fine.'

She wondered if his response was as much a lie as hers. After he left her last night, she had undressed and climbed into bed where she lay awake for hours feeling his kiss imprinted on her lips. Today, her body ached as if from exertion.

She had believed she was immune to a man's kisses, but Tagg had stirred something deep within her. She hadn't wanted to respond—the very idea terrified her—but it was as if her body was acting independently from her mind.

Covertly, she watched Tagg as he scanned the breakfast menu. Clad once more in jeans and a fresh polo shirt, he looked heart-stoppingly vital. He meant

nothing to her—how could he at such short acquaint-
ance? Yet she persisted in noticing small details: the
way his fingers curled around the menu, the nails
surprisingly well kept for a farmer; and the texture and
tightness of his skin which made her long to run a hand
along his forearm.

She should have learned her lesson last night. She
wasn't ready for a man like Tagg Laskin yet, if she ever
would be. What manner of man was he to provoke such
passionate longings in her? Was it only that he was the
very antithesis of Steve?

She gave a shuddering sigh and Tagg, ever alert,
noticed the tremor. 'Are you all right?'

'Yes. Probably a draught from somewhere. Somebody
must have opened a door.' Yes, a door to her memories,
she added inwardly. She fastened her eyes on the menu
and recoiled at the hearty foods on offer. Quickly, she
closed the folder. 'I'll just have coffee and orange juice.'

'You ought to have something more substantial,'
Tagg suggested. 'We won't get to Mundoo until
lunchtime and you'll be sorry then that you didn't have
something now.'

'I'm not a big eater, especially at breakfast.'

He glanced at her thin wrists, which looked as if a firm
grip could snap them in two. 'I'd say you aren't a big
eater at any time. Underweight, aren't you?'

She was, but it was none of his business. 'I'm not one
of your livestock, needing to be conditioned,' she
snapped. 'Orange juice and black coffee,' she said
defiantly to the waitress who came up to them just then.

'And bacon and eggs for two,' Tagg added. 'And a
side order of hash brown potatoes.'

The waitress grinned. 'You never give up, do you, Mr

Laskin? This is Australia, not America.' She winked at Lee. 'I tell him so every time he comes here for breakfast.'

He pretended chagrin. 'Can't blame a man for trying.'

'You're wasting your money ordering food for me,' Lee said crossly when the waitress had gone, 'I shan't eat it.'

A frown crossed his even features. 'Don't you ever do anything without an argument?'

What was the use? He would see for himself when the food arrived. Besides, she had something more important to discuss with him. 'I—I've decided not to come to Mundoo, after all,' she said, plunging in head first.

His eyebrow arched upwards. 'May I ask why you've changed your mind?'

He was being deliberately obtuse. 'You must see why I can't, after . . . after last night.'

A slow smile spread across his face. 'Last night, we had dinner and said goodnight at your door, if I remember correctly.'

'You remember accurately as far as you choose,' she said, holding her temper in check with an effort. 'Let me refresh your memory about the rest. You made some unwelcome advances to me and because I rebuffed them, you threatened to make my life at Mundoo unpleasant. I think it's called sexual harassment these days.'

The smile vanished and his eyes hardened. 'It seems your memory is flawed, too. You were the one who gave me the impression you welcomed my so-called advances. And the only threat I made was to leave you alone. If you consider that a threat, then you *are* playing some sort of game. Or else you don't know what you want, a dilemma for which you can't very well blame me.'

'I'm sorry if I gave you the impression I wanted you to ... to ...' She couldn't go on.

'To make love to you?' he supplied unhelpfully. 'And yes, you did—twice, including the night of Karen's party.'

She spread her hands helplessly. 'Can't you just accept that I'm not right for the job at Mundoo, and let's leave it at that?'

'No, I can't,' he snapped, 'for a number of reasons. One, qualified farm secretaries are as scarce as hen's teeth; and two, I'm up to my ears in work and I haven't the time to go looking for a replacement. If you want a third reason, think about your friend who's depending on you.'

'I can't see how I'm hurting Karen,' she said, bewildered by this line of attack.

'I've worked with Karen Ritchie for four years and I've come to respect her. She built her business out of nothing, but if you let her clients down she'll have no business to return to. Is that how you want to repay her for trying to help you?'

He had given the one reason she couldn't refute. She didn't know what she would have done without Karen over the last year. As well as providing moral support, she had helped Lee to find a place to live and lent her money when Steve closed their joint banking account, meagre though it was, to try to force her to come back to him.

She couldn't destroy Karen's hard work through her own cowardice. 'If I decide to stay?' she said tentatively.

'I gave Karen my word I would accept you. I never go back on my word.'

Did that include his promise last night? she wondered bleakly. She should be grateful to Karen for ensuring that Tagg couldn't change his mind but she almost wished he wasn't so principled. If he had accepted that she wasn't suited to the work, that would have been the end of it. Now she was committed for Karen's sake.

Aware that Tagg was watching her, Lee averted her eyes. Her body had told him the truth—she did want him. But she was too scarred by her past to take the risk. So maybe it was just as well he insisted on a purely business relationship. What other kind could she endure?

They reached Mundoo by mid-afternoon, having stopped on the way to collect the drive shaft Tagg was waiting for.

'I thought you said this was Mundoo,' Lee said after a half-hour of driving along a rutted dirt road flanked by flat, dry sheep paddocks with clusters of merino sheep dotted sparsely over them.

'I did, but we still have some way to go before we reach the homestead. Mundoo Run covers ten thousand hectares.'

He informed her that, as well as the sheep, he had several hundred hectares of wheat, oats and hay for stock feed, and two hundred head of poll shorthorn cattle pastured on the river country.

Lee absorbed all this in silence. Karen had told her that Mundoo was the size of a small town, but she was still unprepared for the reality.

She was even more surprised when the homestead emerged out of the flat scrub, like pictures in a child's pop-up book.

In fact, the homestead was not one building but a cluster of white weatherboard buildings linked together. The main wing, its gables standing above the old cedar trees in the garden, had the date 1880 mounted over the entrance. A covered walkway joined it to a smaller building and gnarled grapevines hung limply from the walkway in the afternoon heat.

A short, stocky man in grey moleskins and checked shirt came out to meet their car.

'G'day, boss!' he called in greeting.

'Ray di Falco, this is our new farm secretary, Alita Perry,' Tagg said formally.

Lee had already guessed the identity of the man and she murmured a response. 'You're the manager here, aren't you?' she added.

'I'm the manager as long as Cheryl isn't home,' he said with a wink. 'She's my wife and she's dying to meet you.'

Instantly, Lee took a liking to the manager and felt a sense of relief. At least she wouldn't be entirely at the mercy of Tagg Laskin while she was here.

She stood quietly in the background while the two men exchanged news and Ray told Tagg what had happened in his absence. Just when Lee wondered if Tagg had forgotten her presence altogether, he interrupted Ray. 'We'll sort the rest out in my office later,' he said. 'I have to get Lee settled in.'

Ray smiled apologetically. 'Sorry, I wasn't thinking. I'll leave you to the boss's tender mercies.'

Resisting an urge to call him back, Lee watched bleakly as he strode away. She caught her sigh of resignation just in time and turned to Tagg. 'Which cottage is to be mine?' There were several small cottages clustered around the main building.

Tagg picked up her suitcases and nudged the flyscreen door open with his foot. 'You'll be sleeping in here and taking your meals with me.'

Lee froze in her tracks. Living under Tagg's roof was something she hadn't bargained for. Knowing she would have her own place had been one of the reasons she'd given in to Karen's entreaties. 'I was told I'd have my own accommodation. I'm quite prepared to pay whatever rent you require,' she said firmly in case he thought she expected something different.

'That was the arrangement I had with Karen,' he agreed. 'But I decided to use the time she's away to renovate her cottage. It needs some new plumbing and wiring and this is a good time to do it. It's larger than the one Ray and Cheryl now have and I plan to let them have it in time for the baby they're expecting.'

He had it all worked out, all except for her. 'I still prefer to be independent,' she said. 'Surely you must have somewhere else I can live?'

His eyes sparkled, but whether with anger or amusement at her attitude, she wasn't sure. 'There's the stables and the cowbails,' he suggested.

'I meant another cottage.'

'They're all occupied.' He shifted impatiently. 'Look, your room is ready here and we've fixed up an office for you next door to mine. What's so terrible about that? I thought you'd be glad to sleep here, out of reach of snakes, spiders and mice.'

Involuntarily, she shuddered. She knew the liabilities of living in the country, having done so most of her life, but she hadn't taken them into account when she pictured herself living alone. 'You could have told me about the new arrangements before we left Walgett,' she said despairingly.

'And you'd have reacted the same way. I was hoping you would see reason once you took a look at your quarters.'

'You mean, you were hoping I'd be too tired to argue,' she retorted.

'Have it your own way. But I'm going inside to put these bloody suitcases down, whether you're coming in or not.'

She had little choice but to follow him inside, although she was still simmering with fury over his high-handed behaviour. He knew she was ambivalent about him—attracted to him yet unwilling to become involved with any man. The last thing she wanted was to share a house with him!

Despite her annoyance, she could see that the homestead was a warm, inviting place. Her first impression was of rich greens and creams which harmonised with the gum trees and peppercorns outside. Opening off the wide hallway was a living-room where the colonial theme was continued in timber, brass and sandstone, softened by richly coloured rugs and cushions on the sofas and armchairs.

The walls of both living-room and hallway were hung with paintings by local artists, some whose names she recognised. She didn't have much time to appreciate the rest of the house before Tagg led her up a staircase to what he announced would be her room.

'I'll leave you to settle in,' he said, and deposited her luggage in the middle of the room, then left before she could argue further.

She looked around, curious in spite of herself. The

sunny bedroom was panelled in warm-hued timber and was furnished with wicker furniture piled with plump cushions. A brass bedstead was covered in a patchwork quilt.

Leading off the room was a glassed-in veranda which was decorated as a sitting-room. It had a pine floor and leaded windows looking out on to the garden.

Another door led to a walk-in wardrobe in which her few possessions would look lost. In turn the dressing-room led to a small private bathroom.

She felt ashamed of her earlier protestations. The room was really more of a suite. Only at mealtimes and during business hours would she need to have much contact with Tagg. She could easily pass her evenings here, reading or sewing, and she was unlikely to tire of the view from her private sitting-room.

All the same, she wished Tagg wouldn't make her decisions for her.

But he was right, she wouldn't have come if she'd known she was to live in his house, she admitted to herself. Annoyed at her own ambivalence, she began to unpack and settle in.

An hour later, after a brief shower and change of clothes to rid herself of the dust of travel, she felt refreshed and curious about the rest of the house. In particular, she wanted to see her new office and read the note Karen had left for her.

Making her way back to the hall, she explored the rooms opening off it. The dining-room, with its carved overmantel, looked out on to the garden. Frosted glass doors connected it to the terrace. Beyond that the kitchen was farmhouse-friendly. Lovely old cedar cupboards and cedar shelves held cooking utensils,

Johnson Brothers china and Tudor Village ironware.

As she explored, she enjoyed the natural coolness of the house in contrast to the brilliant sunshine outside. Since there was no one about, she found her way by trial and error to the building attached by walkway to the main house. It must have been the kitchen block years ago, but was now converted to offices.

The first door Lee opened led to a large, cluttered room with a battered leather-topped desk on which was scattered piles of paper and farm magazines.

On a shelf behind the desk was a row of shiny silver trophies from sheep and cattle shows, and ribbons from the same source adorned the wall on either side.

This must be Tagg's office, she decided, shutting the door quickly. She didn't want him to think she was snooping.

The next office clearly belonged to her. There were two desks in the room, set at right angles to each other. On one was set up a desk-top computer—a model she recognised and would easily be able to use, she thought with relief. A filing cabinet occupied another corner. The room was orderly and, knowing Karen, the files would be in apple-pie order. She had always been much tidier than Lee at school. It was only emotionally that she behaved erratically—as witness her recent elopement.

Lee smiled involuntarily at the thought of Karen, now Mrs Kevin Vaughan, lying on a beach in Fiji with her new husband. A pang very like jealousy shot through Lee. Life was so unfair. She didn't begrudge her friend a minute of her happiness, but she couldn't help wishing she could taste a little of it herself.

Dismissing the thought as useless self-pity, she sat

down at the desk. In the centre was a sealed envelope labelled simply 'Lee'.

She opened it curiously and smiled as she recognised Karen's sharply sloping handwriting. Like the message to Tagg, Lee's note started with an apology.

'I just can't let Mother orchestrate my wedding as if it was one of her charity affairs,' she continued. 'I know this will be difficult for you—we both know why—but I believe you are ready to go solo, otherwise I would never have deserted you. All the same, I feel rotten about it and you can tell me exactly what you think of me when I get back. I owe you that much.'

Lee shook her head as she read the last line. Even if she didn't owe Karen more than she could ever repay, she couldn't reproach her friend for her impulsive act. Karen loved Kevin to distraction. They would have been married long before if Olive Ritchie hadn't urged them to postpone the date while her plans grew more and more ambitious. It was no wonder Karen finally took matters into her own hands.

'Forgive me, Lee,' the letter ended. 'I know you'll be a big success at Mundoo. I have left step-by-step guidelines on the computer for you. I'll be back from my honeymoon before shearing time, which is when things start hotting up, so don't worry.

'When we get back I hope to have a couple of months at home with Kevin getting our new home together, then I'll be ready to take over the reins again—by which time I hope you'll have decided what you want to do. Meantime, you're in good hands at Mundoo. Love, Karen.'

Thinking of how close she had come to letting Karen down, Lee felt terrible. Thank goodness Tagg had

talked her into coming—and staying. It was the only way
she'd learn to stand on her own feet again, as Karen
rightly perceived.

For the first time, she wondered if this was what
Karen had in mind when she decided to elope. Was it
part of some scheme to rescue Lee? It wouldn't be the
only reason, of course, but that kind of thinking was
typical of Karen. If so, Lee had more reason than ever to
make a success of things at Mundoo.

She looked up to find Tagg braced in her doorway,
appraising her intently. She wondered what emotions
she had betrayed to his gaze as she read Karen's letter.
His expression gave her no clues.

'Is the office to your liking?'

Her head came up and she answered him with an
assurance born partly out of Karen's faith in her, and
largely from her own innate stubbornness. 'It's fine,
thank you. I haven't gone through Karen's briefing yet
but it shouldn't take me long to get the hang of things.'

His eyes narrowed. 'I'm pleased to hear it. And the
room?'

'It's more like a suite, actually. And it's lovely.'

When he continued to stare at her, she shifted
restlessly. 'Is something the matter?'

'I'm not sure. You sound . . . different, somehow.'

She tossed her head. 'You're imagining things. It
takes a while to get used to strange surroundings, that's
all.'

'I have a feeling there's more to it than that, but it's
your business. I just want you to know I'm right next
door if you need any help. I keep an open-door policy for
all my people.'

So his offer wasn't especially for her, she thought,

colouring slightly. For a moment, she'd imagined ...
but then, she reminded herself, it was her own fault if he
held himself aloof from her. When he had attempted to
get closer to her, she had rebuffed him—not once, but
twice.

He'd made it quite clear that he was a man of his word.
He'd vowed that she would have to beg him to touch her
again, and nothing was going to make her do that. With
Steve, she'd done enough begging for a lifetime.

Tagg was altogether different from Steve, she
acknowledged. But how could she trust her judgement
again when she'd been so wrong about a man before?

After Tagg excused himself to have his meeting with
Ray di Falco, Lee turned on the computer and spent the
next hour going over Karen's instructions which were
recorded on a floppy disk. The routine was reassuringly
familiar from Lee's college days. Her main tasks were
handling the correspondence, doing the accounting,
filing and ordering for the station, keeping stock and
performance records and a dozen other clerical tasks.
Karen had also worked outside occasionally, drafting
stock, drenching and mustering sheep, but Lee doubted
whether she would have time for such activities during
her stay. If she was lucky, she might find time to go
riding, though. She had always enjoyed riding and had
kept up her skills by riding hired horses even when she
lived in the city. It would be good to get back in the
saddle.

By lunchtime next day, she had a good grasp of what
was required of her. She had also caught up on the
backlog of banking and filing which had accumulated
since Karen had left.

The telephone rang and she yawned and stretched as

she reached to answer it. 'Hello?'

There were no long-distance pips, so it was a local call, but she didn't recognise the female voice which responded. 'I'm Cheryl di Falco,' the woman explained, 'Have you made any plans for lunch today?'

Lee had been wondering what everyone did for lunch at Mundoo. She had forgotten to ask Tagg at dinner last night, and had seen no one around the homestead all morning. 'It's good to speak to you, Mrs di Falco,' she responded. 'As a matter of fact, I was just wondering whether to go raid a refrigerator somewhere.'

'Then come over here and raid mine,' the other woman invited, 'and please call me Cheryl. Mrs di Falco makes me feel old.'

She wasn't old at all, Lee discovered when she walked over to the manager's cottage at the far side of the gardens. Cheryl di Falco was petite and trim with bright hazel eyes and deeply tanned skin, topped by a swirl of lemon-meringue hair. She looked like one of the dolls sold at country fairs. Lee warmed to her at once.

'You didn't have to telephone, you could have dropped in,' she said when she was comfortably seated in the manager's cottage.

'I knew you'd be working and I didn't want to disturb you,' Cheryl explained, 'but I know how lonely it can get up at the homestead by yourself all day with nobody else around.'

'Is it always like that?'

'Mostly. The boss doesn't believe in housekeepers. He thinks grown-ups can do their own fetching and carrying. So he only employs a cook—that's Mouse Napier—and pays one of the other wives to come in and spruce things up once a week. I think it's a legacy of being surrounded by servants when he was growing up in America. He prefers doing things for himself.'

From what she already knew of Tagg Laskin, Lee could believe this last. But one thing Cheryl said nagged at her. 'You said the cook is called "Mouse"—but I met him last night and he must be twenty stone!'

Cheryl laughed. 'You know the Aussie habit—every redhead is called "Blue", and the bigger you are, the more likely you are to be called "Tiny".'

'Or Mouse,' Lee supplied.

The initial shyness well and truly dispelled, the two women were soon talking as if they had been friends for years. Not since Karen and Doctor Mather had Lee found someone she could talk to as easily as Cheryl di Falco. No wonder Karen spoke so highly of her.

'You seem to know everyone around here,' she commented.

'You mean everyone's business,' Cheryl laughed. 'Don't look so worried—I'm not known around here as "Reuters" for nothing. In my case, the nickname is true to form. I can't bear to be left out of anything.'

Since she wasn't sure how to respond to this frank admission, Lee said, 'Karen told me you have a little boy.' She tried to keep the envy out of her voice.

'Oh yes, Craigie. I hope she warned you about him. He's a terror for getting into everything, including Karen's office. He adored her.'

Lee looked around. 'Where is he now?'

'At pre-school.'

'He travels all the way to Walgett?'

Cheryl laughed. 'Oh, no! He would have done, not long ago, though. The station owners around here got together and built a schoolhouse on land that the boss

donated. It's a one-room school where all the grades take
their lessons at the same time. You should visit it while
you're here.'

'I ... I might. We'll see.' This time Lee's voice
betrayed her. She didn't think she could bear visiting a
school full of happy children just yet, especially if any of
them were the age Sally was ... would have been, she
amended with a pang. She had thought she was getting
over her loss a little, but the sight of Cheryl, so happily
pregnant, and her talk about her little boy, was almost
more than she could bear.

'What's the matter? You've gone quite white.' Cheryl
said, interrupting her thoughts.

'I'm all right. It must be the heat,' she improvised.
'Orange, where I grew up, is a lot cooler than around
here.'

Cheryl got up and turned on an air-conditioning unit
which sent a blissful draft of cool air through the room.
'I should have realised you aren't acclimatised yet,' she
apologised.

Lee felt guilty for misleading the other woman. She
was feeling the heat, but not as badly as Cheryl thought.
It was thinking about Sally which had made her go pale.

'You're not married, I take it?' Cheryl said, as if
divining her thoughts.

'No, I was. But it didn't work out.'

'It happens a lot these days,' Cheryl said philosophic-
ally. 'I thank my lucky stars I got the right man first go.'

Unexpectedly, Lee's eyes filled with tears. She looked
away, but not before Cheryl spotted them. 'Did I say
something?'

'No, I was feeling sorry for myself, hearing you talk
about your happy marriage.'

Cheryl leaned forward and touched her hand. 'I hope you haven't written off all marriage just because of one bad experience,' she said earnestly. 'I'm living proof that it can work.'

If she knew just how bad that one experience had been, Lee doubted whether Cheryl would have been so optimistic. 'I'm all right,' she said again. 'The single life has its compensations, too. Like the freedom to come and go as you please—take this job, for instance. I couldn't have taken it on if I was still tied down.'

Cheryl's look said she recognised this as bravado, but she wisely said nothing. Instead, she led Lee to the table where a crisp salad and grilled steaks were waiting.

When Lee commented on the tenderness of the steak and the freshness of the salad, Cheryl said, 'One of the advantages of living on a place this size. Everything you're eating is Mundoo-grown or killed.'

As she ate her steak, Lee tried not to think of the sloe-eyed cattle she'd seen grazing along the river flats. By encouraging Cheryl to talk, she soon learned a great deal about the station and the people who ran it. 'I'm surprised that Tagg Laskin is still single,' she observed, surprising herself with such a blatant quest for information.

Cheryl smiled. 'Don't worry, a lot of the local women have tried to change his status. He's the hottest thing at the B and S balls—that's Bachelor and Spinster,' she explained when Lee looked puzzled. 'For a while, we thought Karen might be the one, but she only had eyes for Kevin Vaughan. Besides, I'm convinced that Tagg is married to the station and his research.'

'The perennial grasses,' Lee said, remembering what Tagg had told her at Karen's party.

'I see you've heard about his pet project. It's valuable work in its way, especially if he can achieve his aim of drought-proofing Mundoo, but it doesn't leave him much time for socialising. Not that his name isn't linked with some heiress or other from time to time.'

Lee recalled Tagg's jocular reference to his 'reputation' which he denied earning. 'I suppose that's mostly unfounded gossip,' she said carefully.

'I wouldn't bet on it. Our Tagg is a normal, virile man. If he's living the life of a monk up there at the big house, I'll be surprised. His dislike of servants may not be the only reason he doesn't have a live-in house-keeper,' she said conspiratorially.

Uncomfortable with the turn the discussion had taken, Lee glanced at her watch. 'I'd better get back to work, but thanks for lunch.'

'Any time. Come over for coffee any morning. Karen often did,' Cheryl urged. She patted her stomach which was barely rounded. 'I'm still pretty mobile with this character, but as he grows I won't get around so easily so I'll need you to keep me up with the news.'

Small communities were the same everywhere, Lee mused as she walked back across the gardens to her office. There was no such thing as a private life. Everyone knew everyone else's business.

Whether the gossip was accurate or not was another matter. Was Tagg a ladies' man as Cheryl suggested, or was he simply the victim of gossip, as he maintained?

To her astonishment, Lee realised she cared which it was. Yet there was no reason why she should. He had made it quite clear that theirs was to be a business relationship from now on, so it didn't matter how many girlfriends he had. She would never be among them.

All the same, her thoughts kept drifting to the subject as she tried to concentrate on her work that afternoon. As dinnertime neared, her mood grew lighter. Surely it couldn't be at the prospect of sharing the meal with Tagg?

She couldn't deny that she was attracted to him. In many ways, the feeling was stronger than it had ever been with Steve. 'All the more reason to watch your step,' she told herself firmly.

Except that reason had nothing to do with the way her pulses raced and her body temperature soared whenever Tagg was around.

CHAPTER FOUR

THREE weeks later, her work finished for the day, Lee sat in her office writing a letter to her parents.

With enforced cheerfulness, she told them about her work and the endless variety of station life. She had plenty to write about with her growing friendship with Cheryl and the rides she had managed to fit in during her busy work day. She also told them about the dust storm Mundoo had endured the previous day.

The heaps of sand swept away from the doors were still piled outside and the potted plants and vines on the veranda hung limply in the oppressive atmosphere. Banks of menacing black clouds built up in the north-west, but when Lee said it looked as if rain was imminent, the station hands shook their heads.

'We've seen clouds like that too often in the last few months, but there's never any decent rain in it,' they told her. 'If we don't get a good downpour soon, we'll have water restrictions this summer.'

Her parents still remembered their days of relying on rainwater tanks and water the colour of tomato juice. They would be interested in these anecdotes.

It was only when Lee came to write about the boss of Mundoo Run that her pen hovered uncertainly over the paper. How could she write about him in platitudes, as if he was no more than another character in her new life?

Because he was a lot more than that.

After dinner last night, she had finally faced the fact

that Tagg Laskin had come to mean something special in her life. It was an admission she had thought never to make about a man again.

True to his word, he had been polite and friendly but nothing more. He had even apologised when his hand brushed her arm as they both reached for the salt at the same time.

Absently, Lee caressed the skin where he had touched it, a smile tilting up the corners of her mouth. He was so gentle and considerate. Maybe she was foolish in denying herself a closer relationship with him.

Briefly she allowed herself to imagine what it would be like to be mistress of Mundoo. She would help Tagg run the property, and the lovely old homestead would be her home.

As his wife, she would share his bed.

'No!'

She was unaware of having cried the word aloud until the door between their offices swung open and Tagg looked in, his expression anxious. 'Is something wrong?'

'No, I ... I'm all right, thanks. I just gave myself a fright.'

He came in and stood across the desk from her, resting his hands on the edge of it so that his face was a short distance from hers. 'You don't look all right. What frightened you?'

'N ... nothing.' How could she admit that it was the prospect of going to bed with him which had made her blood run cold? She had glimpsed herself lying by his side, seeing him reach for her, and the panic had returned as it hadn't done since she came here.

He frowned. 'For nothing, you're looking mighty

pale, even with the tan you've acquired since you got here.'

Weakly, she forced a smile. 'I thought the printer ribbon was a spider sitting on my desk.'

He glanced at the tangled ribbon she'd been about to discard because it had jumped out of its cassette. 'I suppose it does look peculiar, especially if caught out of the corner of your eye. Still, I wouldn't have picked you for a scaredy-cat.'

Thank goodness he believed her hastily invented excuse. 'I'm all right now,' she added to reassure him.

Instead of returning to his office, he dropped into her visitor's chair and poured himself a glass of iced water from the pitcher on her desk. She shook her head in response to his unspoken enquiry. 'I'm not thirsty.'

'Well, I am. I was down taking a look at the big dam this morning and got a lungful of dust. God, I wish this weather would break.'

She waited in silence while he sipped his drink, wondering what he wanted from her. Apart from business, he had barely spoken to her during the day. At mealtimes, they talked of neutral subjects until she was ready to scream.

But wasn't it what you wanted? she asked herself. Her reaction a few minutes ago proved she was far from ready to have a normal relationship with a man—and she was certain that Tagg would settle for nothing less.

She realised he had been speaking to her for some time. 'I'm sorry?'

'You were miles away. I said I have to go over to Robina tomorrow. Since they're among your clients, I thought you might like to go with me.'

Robina was a neighbouring sheep station whose books

Lee looked after. She had managed to visit all of Karen's clients in turn during the last three weeks, but since Robina was furthest away she hadn't yet been to see them.

'I'd like that,' she agreed. 'I've discussed Robina's accounts on the phone with Dave Beeching but it would be nice to meet him face to face.'

Tagg stood up. 'In that case, be packed and ready tomorrow morning. We'll leave after breakfast.'

Puzzlement flickered on her face. 'Packed? Are we staying there overnight?'

'We might have to. I know everyone is saying it won't rain and we've had those cloud banks before, but if it does start we won't make it back here until it stops.'

Alone in her room that evening, Lee looked at her meagre wardrobe in indecision. What did one pack in case one was marooned at a strange sheep station?

Tagg had already warned her at dinner that the road would be dusty, so she laid out her jeans, the ankle boots she used for riding, and a long-sleeved cotton shirt. To change into on arrival, she packed an aqua-coloured jersey dress which travelled well and wouldn't crush. Her white leather sandals and a silver heart-shaped necklace given to her by Karen on a previous birthday completed the outfit.

After a moment's hesitation, she tucked her flannelette nightdress into the case. It wasn't a glamorous garment, but she wanted as much covering as possible in case she had to be seen in the garment at Robina.

Her packing completed, Lee sat on the edge of her bed and stared out through the leaded panes of her veranda, at the gathering dark.

The idea of spending the day with Tagg sent tremors

of anticipation through her and her heart began its now-familiar pounding. Not for the first time, she recalled his kiss at the hotel in Walgett, and she knew she would give a lot to have him kiss her again.

With a shock, she realised she really did want him to hold her in his arms. A shuddering breath escaped her lips as she finally acknowledged how lonely she'd been since her marriage ended.

Impatiently, she picked up her hair brush and brushed her hair with jerky movements. It was ridiculous, to fantasise about Tagg. He wasn't the kind of man to settle for hugs and kisses. And she wasn't able to give him more. So what was the use?

Lee's tension must have shown on her face when she joined Tagg at the Landcruiser next morning, having skipped breakfast as usual.

'Don't look so anxious. I'm used to outback driving,' he reassured her.

'I wasn't worried—I didn't sleep too well last night,' she told him truthfully.

'Well, you can sleep on the way to Robina.' He handed her a plastic container. 'You might need this.'

She looked at it curiously. 'What is it?'

'The breakfast you missed. I had Mouse pack some hard-boiled eggs, tomatoes, cheese and fresh damper for you.'

'You're very kind,' she said, meaning it.

His brow crinkled into a frown. 'You're always telling me how kind I am. You make yourself sound like a stray animal I've generously taken in.'

Although she did appreciate the job, she didn't feel quite *that* grateful, but made a mental note not to annoy him again by calling him kind. She hadn't realised she'd made a habit of it.

An hour along the track, the rain Tagg had anticipated started. It was so quiet and gentle at first that Lee thought she was imagining the blurring of the windscreen, then she glanced across at Tagg to find him grinning broadly. 'It's starting, honey. It's finally starting!'

He was right. Gradually the drops grew heavier until they formed a solid sheet which settled into a soaking downpour.

Around them, the thirsty earth soaked it up. As they drove across creek beds, their wheels churned up the warm, dry gravel underneath the moist topsoil. On the flat, puddles formed in their wheeltracks, the first water the ground had known for months.

'Doesn't it smell fantastic?' Tagg asked her, laughter in his voice.

She nodded. The smell of the moist earth was rich and fruity, like new-mown grass and Christmas pudding all mixed together. Tagg wound his window down and thrust his arm out into the downpour and Lee followed his example, revelling in the coolness of the rain on her skin. When they pulled in at the drafting yards to look at a mob of sheep a jackeroo had mustered by motorbike, Tagg and the stockmen walked happily around in the rain. Lee got out and joined them, sharing their joy at this replenishment of the dry earth.

When Tagg returned to the car, his smile mirrored hers. 'The men tell me the creek's running into the big dam by now. If we get eight feet into her, that'll see us through to the middle of next year.'

They travelled on in contented silence, the drumming

of the rain on the car roof too loud for normal
conversation. Only when they crossed a shallow gravel
bed more than ten metres across, and their wheels
bogged in the sloppy sand and gravel surface, did she
start to worry.

'Will we make it to Robina?' she called over the
drumming of the rain.

Tagg gave all his attention to the driving but
answered out of the side of his mouth. 'Your guess is as
good as mine.'

'You mean we might not?'

'I mean I don't know,' he shouted back. He pointed to
another of the gravel creek beds some distance ahead.
'That starts about forty kilometres away in the Ranges.
If they get a couple of inches of rain there, it'll be down
here in a flash flood. That's the sort of thing we have to
worry about.'

When he prophesied rain, she had no idea it would
transform the countryside so quickly, or make it so
hazardous. Friendly flats, which could have been
traversed at a bumpy but fast speed, were now
treacherous mud flats which had to be crossed with care.
Even then, their vehicle slipped and slid alarmingly.

The rain no longer seemed so benevolent as it
continued to pound relentlessly on the roof. Around
them, the earth took it up gratefully and the corellas
patrolling the creek beds whistled their thanks.

Lee's fingernails dug into her palms as she tried to
avoid thinking the unthinkable—that she might be
marooned out here, alone with Tagg.

Just when she had decided they might make it after
all, the dust-dry track ahead turned into a morass. Even
a four-wheel-drive vehicle would have trouble fording

it. After several valiant tries, Tagg brought the car to a halt and looked gloomily at the mess ahead. 'We'll have to wait it out.'

'You mean spend the night here?' she asked, although she already knew the answer.

'There's a boundary rider's hut across that paddock,' Tagg said, gesturing. 'We'll get wet on the way but it's better than trying to sleep in the car.'

She nodded. Anything was better than that. Following his lead, she took her small overnight bag out of the back seat and jumped out into the grey mud.

They squelched their way across the paddock until the cabin Tagg was seeking came into view. It was a small weatherboard building, the timbers grey with age. As they approached it, Tagg stopped to inspect an old rain gauge on the outside. 'Eighty-five points,' he told her.

She gathered that this was a lot of rain, especially in the short time it had been falling. But all she wanted right now was to be inside and dry. Her shirt clung to her back, outlining every contour of her body, and her shoes squelched with every step. She was shivering violently.

Inside the hut, Tagg pulled sacking away from the windows and let in the grey light. 'Better?' he asked. A kerosene lamp hung from a nail on the wall and Tagg lifted it down, placing matches from his pocket alongside it.

She couldn't speak for the chattering of her teeth, and only nodded.

Seeing her shivers, he said, 'You'd better get out of those wet things before you catch pneumonia. You did bring some dry clothes with you?'

'Y ... yes,' she stammered, then began to laugh. When he asked her what was so funny, she said, 'A n . . . nightdress and a p . . . party dress!'

'I see what you mean. Well, the nightdress should keep you warmest so you'd better put that on. I'll get a fire going to dry us off.'

The hut was intended for overnight camping, she gathered from the makeshift furnishings. There was only one room containing a wooden bedstead, a table and two chairs. She coughed as smoke began to issue from Tagg's embryo fire. 'Where shall I get changed?'

He answered without turning round. 'In here. I shan't look.'

She looked at his broad back, hunched over the fireplace. The idea of changing here, with Tagg only feet away, sent a shaft of fear surging through her. Yet if she didn't get out of her wet clothes, she would come down with something. She had no choice.

Fighting her rising panic, she pulled off her shirt, tearing a button in the process, and reached for her bag. The zipper resisted her icy fingers and she gasped as a hand closed over hers. 'Here, let me.'

She crossed her arms over her chest in a futile attempt to hide her heaving breasts from him. He seemed impervious to her and merely handed her the flannelette nightdress. 'Is this what you were looking for?'

She tried to match his impersonal attitude. 'Yes, thank you.' She was about to pull the garment over her head when he stopped her.

'Hadn't you better take your bra off as well? It's soaking and will soon soak your dry nightdress.'

As she stood there woodenly, unable to move, he became impatient. 'What's the matter with you? Get undressed for God's sake, then give me some room to do the same.'

His impatience broke the spell which transfixed her. He was so clinically detached about their situation that her fear seemed foolish. With stiff fingers, she undid her bra and let it drop, then pulled on the cosy nightdress, feeling warmth flood through her. 'I'm ready,' she said in a subdued tone.

'Great. There isn't much floor space here so it's better if we don't try to change at the same time,' he explained.

Good grief! He was going to follow her example and strip off his wet clothes right here in front of her. 'Isn't there another room here?' she asked miserably.

'I thought you'd been married. Haven't you ever seen a man without his clothes before?' he asked irritably.

The suppressed annoyance in his speech reached Lee and she shrank. The last few times she'd been with Steve when he got that tone in his voice it had been a prelude to pain and fear. She flinched unwittingly, and curled up in the furthest corner of the bed to put as much distance between them as possible.

Through a haze she saw Tagg peel off his sodden shirt and drop it on the chair in front of the fire. The flames flickered off his bronzed skin and its covering of fine dark hairs. Then he came over to where Lee was lying on the bed and put a hand on her shoulder, and she was no longer in the boundary rider's hut, marooned by the torrential rain. She didn't hear what he said. She was back in Sydney and it was happening all over again.

'Please—leave me alone,' she moaned feebly. 'What have I said? I didn't mean to upset you——'

'You little bitch! You're always sorry afterwards, aren't you, always whining!' Steve advanced towards her and raised his hand, and she twisted her face away, feeling humiliation and fear. Yet she couldn't scream, for fear of disturbing Sally, asleep in the next room. She was only two and so ill. Didn't Steve care about any of that?

But he only cared about himself and whatever it was that had sparked his anger this time. She couldn't, she wouldn't go through this again! She fought him, raking the air with her fingernails until she found his face. Her fingers came away bloodied.

'Why, you little . . .'

The pain-filled curse brought her back to reality. She was crouched on the wooden bedstead and Tagg was standing beside the bed, wearing only his trousers. His hand was clutched to his face and she could see traces of blood between his fingers.

She thrust her knuckles into her mouth in horror. 'Oh God, what did I do?'

'When I came towards you and touched you, you went into some sort of trance. Then when I asked you what was wrong, you screamed at me and raked my face with your nails.'

He dropped his hand and she winced at the clear path of scratches her attack had left on his face. 'I'm sorry,' she whispered.

'You're sorry! I'm sorry I didn't keep driving. I had no idea what sort of vixen you were, or even who you thought I was for that matter. Who was I, Alita?'

She shook her head. 'N . . . nobody. I was frightened, that's all.'

His gaze was unrelenting. 'Frightened of whom? Who was I for you just then?'

When she tried to look away, he grasped her wrists and half-hauled her across the bed until she was on her knees facing him. 'You might as well tell me. We've got all night.'

His fingers encircled her wrists like clamps. How could she tell him the truth, knowing his concern would turn to pity or disgust once he knew? She felt the beginnings of tears prickle her eyes and looked aside.

'Damn it all!' He dropped her wrists and sat down on the bed beside her. 'Why do you make me feel like a hulking great brute? Even when you're the one marking me for life, I end up feeling like it's my fault.'

Since she had no answer for him, she kept silent as he stood up and paced across the cabin. His back was broad and his shoulders sloped to muscled arms. His skin was bronzed from the sun, and she felt a sudden longing to run her hands across his back.

Suddenly he turned and faced her. 'I can't get to first base with you, it seems.'

'I didn't think you wanted to any more.'

'Neither did I, but seeing you every day at Mundoo has made me realise how much I'm attracted to you.' Balling his fist, he pressed it against the open palm of his other hand, 'Damn it, I was going to make you beg me to touch you, but now I'm on the verge of begging *you* for that right.' He laughed harshly. 'God, how my friends and family back in Texas would laugh at the idea of Taggart Burnett Laskin on his knees to a woman!'

The realisation of what this admission must have cost him shook her. While she had been imagining what it would be like to be in his arms, he had been fantasising about her. It seemed inconceivable that he could care so much. 'You don't have to beg, you know,' she said carefully.

He regarded her steadily, tension in every line of his

body. 'Are you saying you could care for me?'

'I have done, ever since we met. I'm just not ... not very good at expressing my feelings.'

His look changed to one of appeal. 'Is that why you won't tell me why you look so frightened every time I come near you?'

She twisted the coarse wool blanket between her fingers. 'It's not that I won't; I ... I can't. And it isn't you I'm frightened of.'

'Then what is it, for God's sake?'

In an agony of indecision, she leaned against the cabin wall, smelling the dust and cobwebs and the mustiness of the blanket on the old bed. Her legs were twisted under her and she grasped her ankles, straining to find words to explain herself to him.

She was still marvelling at the discovery of his feelings for her. It was as if someone had given her an incredibly fragile treasure. How could she destroy it with a few words? Yet that's all it would take to turn her precious bauble into dust. In despair, she covered her face with her hands.

Instantly, Tagg was at her side, kneeling on the dusty floor-boards to clasp her in his arms.

With a muffled cry, she tried to pull free, but his hold tightened. 'Sssh ... Sssh ... Don't fight me, I won't hurt you,' he said, his voice gentle, as if he was talking to a frightened colt.

He brushed her hair back from her face with one hand, keeping the other around her shoulders. 'There, it's all right, isn't it?'

Trembling from head to foot, she nevertheless managed to hold still in his arms and nodded weakly. 'Yes.'

'That's better. That's my girl.'

For long minutes, he just held her, not tightening his hold but not freeing her either. Waves of panic assailed her and she fought them back. This wasn't Steve, it was Tagg, and she cared for him. She ... she loved him.

Wonderingly, she stared up at him, her eyes wide. It was true. The strange, marvellous feeling she had for Tagg was love.

As if he read her mind, he brought his lips against her forehead and kissed her, his touch butterfly-light. 'You've stopped trembling.'

And she had. How could she be frightened when she was in the arms of the man she loved?

His lips roved over her forehead and she lifted her face as if to the sun's rays. But when his mouth found hers and he began to kiss her in earnest, the old panic returned and she struggled. She couldn't give herself to another man so entirely, trust him so completely, make herself vulnerable all over again.

'Please, don't.'

Instantly, he let her go but still kept an arm around her. 'Don't what—make love to you? Is that what you don't want?'

Dumbly, she nodded. He had his answer in any case, from the rigid way she held herself in his grasp.

'Then the answer is simple,' he said softly, 'I won't make love to you.'

She felt as if she had been given a reprieve. At the same time, she felt a flash of disappointment. 'You won't?'

'Nope. I'll just hold you and we'll talk, but I won't do anything you don't want me to. Is that all right?'

Grateful tears brimmed her eyes. 'Yes, it's all right.'

'Good, fine.' He leaned against the wall, drawing her

back with him until they were both braced against the timber. 'Lee, I know there's something in your past that has turned you off sex. No, don't talk for a minute,' he instructed when she tried to interrupt. 'God knows how I'll do it, but I won't try to make love to you until you're ready. How do you think I feel when you flinch away from me as if I'm about to beat you?'

'I don't want to be like that.'

'But it goes deeper than conscious will. So you need to relearn your responses to a man's touch, starting now. OK?'

Uncertainly, she nodded. 'OK.'

At first, it took every ounce of willpower she possessed not to leap from his arms. But gradually, as his touch remained light, she relaxed.

Her breathing, quick and shallow at first, slowed as he caressed her back and shoulders. His touch was like a feather being drawn over her skin and she shivered, but this time with pleasure.

'Are you all right?' he asked, noticing the tremor.

'Mmmm, yes,' she murmured, lost in the wonder of being touched by a man and enjoying it.

Slowly, imperceptibly, his hand moved down her body until his fingers rested lightly on top of her thighs. She could feel the heat of them through the fabric of her nightdress. She shifted closer to him until their legs, stretched out in front of them on the bed, were touching, and a thrill surged through her.

He turned her sideways until she was in his arms, and his lips brushed her earlobe and continued in a slow trail down the side of her neck. She nuzzled her face into his shoulder.

His hand rested on the small of her back and pulled

her very slightly against him, but this time she didn't resist, finding that she didn't want to. Almost of their own accord, her arms crept up his body and entwined around his neck.

Her nightdress had ridden up as they embraced, and his hand slid under the material, until he spanned the top of her thigh with his fingers. Carefully he slid a hand between her legs and let it rest there.

Her breathing quickened in response and her muscles tensed, ready for flight, as she waited for his next move. But the moment stretched into several and still he lay beside her, his hand resting on her warm skin. A fiery sensation started up in the pit of her stomach and she realised with amazement that she *wanted* him to do more. He was so gentle and patient that she had forgotten to be frightened.

'Oh God, Tagg,' she moaned softly.

Bewilderingly, he suddenly rolled away and came to his feet beside the bed. He moved stiffly, his breathing as fast and shallow as hers.

She watched as he went to the table and lit the kerosene lamp. 'What's the matter?'

He turned back to her and she saw that he was as aroused as she was. 'If I'm to keep my promise about not making love to you, I think we'd better eat,' he said.

She tried to match his cheerful attitude. 'Eat what? I didn't think they kept supplies here.'

'You're forgetting your breakfast.'

From her overnight bag, he pulled out the plastic container of boiled eggs, cheese and damper he had packed before they left. He set out half for each of them on paper napkins, then to her astonishment, pulled a bottle of Riesling out of his own knapsack.

'Where did you get that?'

'Actually, it's a gift for our hostess at Robina, but I think Stella Beeching will forgive us if we drink it, under the circumstances.'

He opened the bottle with a corkscrew attached to his penknife. She accepted a cracked enamel mug and let him pour some of the wine into it for her. 'Here's to Stella Beeching!'

He lifted his own mug. 'Here's to the most beautiful girl in the Outback.'

She felt the colour creeping over her cheeks. 'I'm not sure I deserve such a compliment.'

'Will you stop running yourself down? I don't know how or why you acquired such an inferiority complex, but it's time you realised your own value.'

'I wasn't much value to you just now.'

He put his cup down and regarded her sternly. 'Now stop that. I told you I'm prepared to wait—as long as necessary. When you're ready, you'll tell me what happened to make you so frightened of men.'

Would she ever be ready? She doubted it, but blessed him for his faith in her. 'You're kind . . . kind of special,' she added as his eyes narrowed.

'Just as well you said that.'

They finished their meal in companionable silence as the darkness gathered around them. The rain kept up its steady drumming on the roof, although it wasn't as loud as before. They were able to talk without shouting, and Lee soon found herself exchanging philosophies with Tagg, seeing another, mellower side to him. She discovered that he cherished freedom for all things, and shared her concern for the environment, and love of travel. It seemed the strong attraction they felt for each other was backed by a solid base of shared pleasures and concerns. At last, Tagg said, 'It's getting late. Since we aren't getting out of here tonight, we'd better go to bed. To sleep,' he added firmly.

To further reassure her, he made a bolster out of one of the blankets and placed it between them on the bed. They slept on either side, rolled in more blankets.

Sometime during the night, Lee stirred to find that it was quiet. 'The rain's stopped,' she murmured.

Tagg's arm came across her and she curled her hand over it. 'I know, go back to sleep,' he said.

Reassured by his presence, she did.

CHAPTER FIVE

'DAVE and Stella Beeching are really likeable people,' Lee observed two days later as they drove back across the rutted roadway towards Mundoo, their business at Robina completed.

They passed the boundary rider's hut where they had spent such an extraordinary night, and she looked at it fondly. She wondered if Tagg was also remembering. He hadn't mentioned their strange evening since they had left the hut.

They had awoken to find the drab landscape miraculously transformed with mile after mile of rain-born wild flowers. Seeds which had been dormant in the ground for months had sprung to colourful life. The saltbush and bluebush, which provided permanent feed for the stock, were freshened and nutritious. In a short time, there would be green grass knee-high, Tagg told her.

By the time they emerged from the hut, the rain gauge showed a hundred and thirty-five points, enough to put millions of gallons of water into the dams dotted around the countryside.

When they finally reached Robina, the Beechings were as jubilant as the other farmers and the radio telephone lines buzzed with news of the good rainfalls everyone had experienced.

'We'll be mating a good line of ewes this season,' Dave Beeching told her enthusiastically, explaining that this meant a profitable lambing season ahead and future stocking made safe.

After contacting Mundoo to assure everyone they were safe, Tagg and Lee had joined in the general celebrations at Robina. Getting stranded was common enough in the Outback, where rain could transform a road into a morass in minutes, so no one had been seriously worried.

Although the Beechings laughed with them when they described their rough night in the cabin, Lee was conscious of Stella's curious stares. She was probably wondering about the relationship between Lee and Tagg.

What would they say if they knew how innocently the night had actually been passed?

She looked sidelong at Tagg. He had been more understanding than she had any right to expect, denying his own desires so that she was reassured. Next morning, he had avoided mentioning the previous night, and had talked and laughed with her as if nothing untoward had occurred. I love you, she thought, and smiled.

He looked around at that moment. 'What's so amusing?'

'I was thinking nice thoughts,' she said unhelpfully.

He grinned back. 'As long as they were of me.'

Her spirits soared. Maybe given enough time, they could have a future together, if only she could get over her stupid fears. At least now, she had a powerful incentive.

'Did you get everything you wanted at Robina?' Tagg asked.

He was referring to the administrative details she had to clear up with the Beechings. She had spent several hours working in their office, catching up on the backlog of paperwork, while Dave showed Tagg the breeding stock he had come to inspect. 'Almost everything,' she said with mock seriousness.

He looked at her in astonishment. 'My God, the woman's flirting with me!'

She felt her skin colouring. 'Yes, I am, aren't I?' she said, surprised. It was the first time she had done such a thing in years—and it felt good.

There was a lot of work awaiting them both after the rain and their extended trip to Robina, so Lee had her hands full in her office for the first few hours after they got back.

Tagg went straight back out on to the property with Ray di Falco to check on the dam levels, but she heard him return to his office during the afternoon. Once or twice, Lee looked up at the closed door, imagining him on the other side of it, working at his desk. Was he thinking of her, as she kept thinking of him?

She had never suspected that a man could be so loving and thoughtful. The night with Tagg had been the most precious of her life. She could hardly believe it had really happened. Tagg had held her and kissed her, and she had allowed it, even though she was still unable to respond fully. Maybe in time that would change.

It had to change, she told herself firmly. A man like Tagg would never settle for half a woman.

Her telephone buzzed and she picked it up, finding it was Cheryl, calling to ask if she wanted to take a coffee break.

'Just give me a minute to file these documents on to disk and I'll be right there,' she said happily. In three weeks, she had become very fond of Cheryl. For all her unashamed curiosity, Cheryl was a friendly, outgoing woman who could keep a secret if she had to. Overcoming the sadness of memory, Lee had started knitting for the new baby, although she still felt a pang every time she looked at the tiny garments.

'How was everything at Robina?' Cheryl asked when Lee was seated in the manager's cottage with a cup of coffee and a plate of home-made scones in front of her.

'Hectic,' Lee admitted. 'I wanted to get as far ahead with their book-keeping as I could, in case it's a while before I can get over there again.'

'I didn't mean the station,' Cheryl said impatiently. 'I mean the important matters—like what colour is Stella's hair now, and is their daughter still seeing that good-looking stockman, Jimmy What's-his-name?'

Lee laughed. 'You're incorrigible!' But she went on to indulge Cheryl with all the details she craved, ending with the titbit that not only was the Beechings' daughter still seeing her stockman, but they were expected to announce their engagement any day now.

'I knew it!' Cheryl said with satisfaction. 'Those two are made for each other. Speaking of which,' she leaned forward, 'I believe you and the boss spent an interesting night together during the rains.'

At the inference that she and Tagg were 'made for each other', Lee blushed furiously. 'It wasn't interesting, it was miserable,' she said. 'The road was impassable so we camped in the boundary rider's hut between here and Robina.'

'So what happened?'

'Nothing *happened* as you put it. You make it sound as if Tagg took the first opportunity to ... to ...'

'Race you off,' Cheryl supplied. 'You mean he

didn't?' She rolled her eyes heavenwards. 'My, my, his reputation is slipping.' She looked at Lee keenly. 'Unless . . . you wouldn't be keeping something from me, would you?' Lee's heightened colour was answer enough. 'He *did* try something! The point is, did he succeed?'

'Cheryl! Look, I'd really rather not talk about it.'

'Whatever you say, Lee.' All the same, Lee could see the other woman wasn't convinced. By her silence, Lee had probably added fuel to the fire of Tagg's 'reputation'.

Well, there was nothing she could do about it. Nothing had happened between her and Tagg during the rains and that was that.

But it wasn't for want of trying, a small voice inside her added. If she had been able to respond to Tagg's advances, she was sure he would have made love to her at the cabin.

Deliberately, she steered the conversation on to other topics. After half an hour, she refused Cheryl's offer of more coffee and stood up. 'I have to get back to the office.'

At the door of the cottage, Cheryl paused. 'Oh, I almost forgot. While you were gone, there was a man here asking about you.'

Lee's heart thumped in her chest. 'A man?'

'Sure. A gorgeous hunk with jet-black hair and a moustache. I guessed he was a relative of yours when he said his name was Steve Perry. I told Tagg to tell you, but he must have forgotten to give you the message.'

So that was why Tagg had ridden off soon after they returned, she thought miserably. He must think she was still using him to make her ex-husband jealous.

He couldn't know how wrong he was. The discovery

that Steve had traced her to Mundoo filled her with horror. She had almost convinced herself he had given up and accepted their divorce as final. But he couldn't have if he was still looking for her. Maybe there was another reason, she thought, hoping against hope.

'Did he say what he wanted?' she asked.

'I'm afraid not. I got the impression he was keen to see you, though. He was very annoyed when I told him you were away for a couple of days.'

'Did you tell him when I was due back?'

'I couldn't. It depended on the rain, didn't it?'

Lee hugged Cheryl impulsively, earning a look of surprise from her. 'Bless you!'

Hurrying back across the gardens towards her office, she skirted the smaller building and went straight to the main house, where she headed for her own room.

There she threw herself on to her bed, her mind in a turmoil. Her first impulse was to pack her things and get away from Mundoo before Steve came back. But there was nowhere to go, except to Walgett if she could get someone to drive her there or lend her a car. And Walgett was the most likely place for Steve to be staying.

Somehow, she knew he was still in the area. He hadn't traced her this far to turn around and go back to Sydney without seeing her. Why wouldn't he accept that it was over between them and leave her alone?

She tensed as a knock sounded on her door. 'Who is it?'

'It's me, Tagg. Can I come in?'

Slowly, she got up and opened the door, then turned away before he could see the traces of tears on her cheeks. But he sensed her distress and turned her to face him. 'You look upset. What's the matter?'

'Didn't Cheryl tell you that there's a man here asking about me?'

'Yes, I meant to give you the message but it slipped my mind. Is he the reason why you're so upset?'

Dumbly, she nodded.

'Who is he, Lee, this Steve Perry—a relative of yours?'

There was no way to avoid the answer. 'He's my ex-husband.'

'I see.'

She gave him a look of appeal. 'It isn't what you think. I wasn't trying to make him jealous to bring him back to me.'

'I didn't think anything of the sort.'

She could hardly believe it. 'You didn't? Then why did you rush off as soon as you knew he'd been here?'

'You silly fool! I had a cow in calf that needed my attention. I didn't even know who Steve Perry was, except obviously, some relative of yours. Is that why you're upset? You thought I had misunderstood the reason for his visit?'

She was tempted to tell him the real reason for her distress but it was still too soon. How could she destroy his respect for her by telling him the truth about her marriage? 'Yes, that's it,' she agreed, hating herself for the lie. But it was better than having him despise or pity her. She didn't know which would be hardest to endure.

Mollified, Tagg took her by the shoulders. She fought down her instinctive reaction and stood quietly, his hands resting on her shoulders. 'I came to tell you something,' he explained. 'I have to go away for a few days on a muster.'

'A few days?' she repeated uncertainly. Why did he

have to go away now of all times?

'It won't be for long. But one of the men is ill and we're short-handed so I have to go myself. You'll have lots of company here with Mouse to cook for you, and the di Falcos.' He ran a hand through his untidy thatch of sun-bleached hair. 'I hate going away just now, when we're really starting to get to know one another.'

'Then let me come with you,' she suggested.

'I can't. We've had women on musters before, so it isn't male chauvinism, but this time we want to make it as short a job as possible so we'll be sleeping rough. I don't want to waste time making and breaking camps. I'd hate to put you through that.'

She forced an expression of cheer into her face. She didn't want him distracted by worrying about her, possibly coming to harm because of it. 'I'll be all right, honestly.'

'Are you sure?'

'Of course. As you say, it's only for a couple of days.' With any luck, Steve wouldn't even come back in that time, she added inwardly.

'By the way, what did Steve Perry want?' Tagg asked casually.

Me, she thought miserably. He can't bear the thought of losing one of his possessions so he keeps after me and after me, convinced I'll see reason and come back to him. Aloud she said, 'He didn't say. Some clerical detail of our joint property or something.'

Tagg looked at her keenly. 'As long as he isn't bothering you. I'd kill any man who did that.'

He meant it, she thought with a rush of affection for him. 'I love you,' she said. There! She'd spoken it aloud.

Tagg's grin was bright enough to illuminate her room

all by itself. 'You mean that?'

'I found out at the cabin the other night. I'm only sorry I couldn't show you how I felt.'

'Don't be silly. I knew you felt something for me. I sure as heck feel the same way, which is why I'm not about to rush you. You've already got the wrong notion about men somehow, and I mean to convince you differently. Until I do, I promise you don't have to do anything you don't want to.'

They moved towards each other as if pulled on invisible strings. The gentleness in his expression quieted her rising fear and she went to him willingly. A few inches apart, they stopped and gazed intently into each other's eyes. In the end it was Lee who took the last, inevitable step.

As she came up against him, Tagg's arms went around her and he crushed her tightly to him. 'Oh, Lee!'

This time she felt only a soaring elation that she was in his arms at last. She lifted her face and he sought her mouth with unerring ease, nibbling at her lips as if he was afraid to kiss her fully and scare her off.

Impatient with his teasing kisses, she surprised herself by capturing his mouth with her lips and increasing the pressure until he was forced to kiss her deeply.

As he did so, the fiery sensation returned to her stomach and her muscles automatically tightened. Against her taut stomach she felt him stirring in response. She wanted to go on kissing him for ever, deeper and deeper, until they drowned in the pleasure of it.

With a growl of impatience, he dropped his hand from the small of her back to her hips and lifted her effortlessly into his arms.

Delightedly, she linked her arms around his neck and laughed like a child. 'I thought you said you had to leave.'

'There's no particular hurry,' he said gruffly.

With a rush of the old panic, she realised he meant to make love to her right here and now. She began to struggle in his arms but he held her tightly until they reached the bed, then he lowered her on to it.

But instead of undressing her or himself, as she expected, he stretched out beside her, still fully clothed. He slid one arm under her shoulders and brought her close to him, then with his free hand, he began to caress her with unhurried strokes.

She closed her eyes, marvelling at the sensations which washed over her. She shivered, yet she was feverishly hot. She wanted him to stop, yet perversely she didn't want this heady stimulation to end.

Beside her, Tagg's breathing quickened and his hands felt hot against her skin. He had undone her jeans and his hand rested inside the waistband, his fingers fiery through the thin film of her bikini briefs. Aroused almost beyond endurance, she rolled on to her side and clasped her arms around him. 'Love me, please, Tagg. I ... I want you so much.'

Carefully, he removed his hand from her jeans and slid the zipper closed. 'I made you a promise, remember? I wouldn't do anything you didn't want me to.'

'But I do want you to,' she said, confused.

'At this moment, you don't know what you want. Even as you beg me to make love to you, you're trembling from head to foot. You think you want me, but you aren't ready for that yet.' He pushed the damp strands of hair back from her forehead. 'My poor little

Lee! Will you ever trust me enough to stop shaking whenever I take you in my arms?'

Damn her body for betraying her! He was right. If he had tried to take her now, she would probably have run screaming from the room. 'I'm trying,' she said simply.

'Then stop trying so hard. Just let your feelings guide your body.'

He sat up and swung his legs over the side of the bed. 'I'd better be going. You may not be ready but I sure as hell am.'

'Oh, Tagg, this is so unfair to you,' she said abjectly. How long could he go on subduing his own male urges to humour her?

He grinned wryly. 'I'll live. Besides, I don't expect to be this heroic indefinitely.'

It was a clear warning to her that he intended to make love to her before much longer. Not long ago, the idea would have terrified her. Now she found she was impatient for the moment to arrive. She sat up in the bed and clasped her arms around her knees. 'I hope I'll be worth the wait.'

His teasing expression grew serious. 'You undervalue yourself, Lee. You'll make a wife any man would be proud to acknowledge.'

Any man except Steve Perry, she thought bleakly. He had called her frigid and worse—he had made her start to doubt her own femininity. But Tagg was slowly changing that. Fondly, she watched him combing his unruly hair at her dresser mirror. How much longer must she wait before she could be wholly his?

On his way out of the door, he looked back. 'Take care of yourself while I'm gone. I've given Mouse strict instructions to cook big meals for you and stand over you while you eat them.'

'You're a bully, you know that?' she laughed, and aimed her pillow at the door. But it landed harmlessly against the wood as he closed the door in time. Slowly it opened a crack and Tagg peered around it. 'Missed me!'

She had no more pillows to throw so she made a mock charge at him from the bed. The door closed quickly again and this time she heard his footsteps disappearing down the corridor.

Jumping up from the bed, she ran to the glassed-in veranda in time to see him emerging from the house. His Landcruiser was parked outside and Mouse was just loading some belongings into the back. The two men exchanged a few words then Tagg got into the car and started the engine.

As if he guessed she was watching, he looked upwards and gave her a cheery salute as he started off down the driveway. She returned the gesture, then sank on to one of the wicker chairs, her heart heavy. He had said he wouldn't be gone for long, but even minutes felt too long now. She wished that she had been able to let him make love to her before he left. Then she could hug his possession to her like a gift. But all she had was a sensation of emptiness.

She listened to the sound of his car engine until it died into the distance, then she got up and went downstairs to her office. At least she could lose herself in work while he was away.

As Tagg had promised, Mouse went to great trouble to cook delicious meals for her. If the big, friendly man hadn't been so persuasive, she doubted whether she would have eaten at all during Tagg's absence.

But Mouse gave her no choice. He served her great

steaks of succulent beef from Mundoo's own cattle, and piled her plate with home-grown vegetables. When she protested that she couldn't eat so much, he smilingly reminded her that it was 'boss's orders'.

If the boss had told him to starve and beat her, would he have been so obedient, she wondered good-humouredly? It seemed that Karen was right—on a property, the word of 'the boss' was law.

During the next two days, she missed Tagg more than she would have believed possible. Her days passed quickly enough, as she busied herself with the station's administration. When she was up to date with Mundoo's paperwork she had Karen's other clients to look after, and an overdue letter to write to her parents, so the daytime hours flew by.

The evenings were the worst. She spent the first one with Cheryl and Ray, but didn't want to impose so she excused herself when they invited her to join them again. 'I have to wash my hair,' was her excuse.

In fact she did want to style her hair. Tagg hadn't said how many days he would be gone, but she wanted to look nice for his return, which must be any time now.

It was late and Mouse had returned to his own cottage for the evening, leaving her alone in the homestead, when she heard a car drive up. Her heart leapt. Tagg was back!

When she peered down into the darkness, she could see nothing beyond the dim outline of the car roof and the silhouette of a man emerging from the driver's seat. Hurriedly, she ran down the hallway to greet him at the door.

Pausing at the hall mirror to fluff her hair into place,

she flung the door open, then froze as she saw who stood there. 'Steve!'

The wide, confident smile she remembered, spread across his even features. 'Yeah, it's me. Glad to see me, I'll bet.'

'You know I'm not. I never wanted to see you again!'

He leaned against the doorframe with apparent indolence but he had casually thrust one foot between door and jamb so she couldn't shut him out. 'You don't mean that,' he said.

'What does it take to convince you that our marriage is over?'

His face darkened. 'I won't ever accept it, Lee. You became my wife "till death us do part", remember?'

Trust him to use the marriage vows against her now! 'There was also something about loving, honouring and cherishing me and our child. I don't recall you doing that.'

'You got the treatment you wanted and deserved.'

Her lip curled into a sneer. 'No one deserves the sort of treatment I got from you. It didn't take me long to discover that all marriages weren't like ours. If it hadn't been for Sally, I would have left you long before.' She turned aside. 'Will you go away and leave me alone?'

He looked at her pleadingly. 'Don't turn me away, Lee. I ... I need your help.'

Lights were coming on in the cottages across the compound as people looked to see who the visitor was. Unlike Lee, they hadn't mistaken the sound of the rental car's engine for Tagg's vehicle. 'You'd better come inside,' she said wearily.

Seeing him standing across the room, her old fear returned. She shouldn't have allowed him in. To disguise her uneasiness, she went to Tagg's bar and poured herself a sherry. She almost never drank it but it was the easiest to hand. She couldn't let him see how badly her hands were shaking, by trying to open another bottle. Steve had always been angered even further by her fear of him.

'Yes, thank you, I'd love a drink,' he said sarcastically.

Deliberately, she had avoided offering him one, but now it was easier to pour a second glass and hand it to him. He took it and tossed it back in one gulp, his eyes fixed on her.

His unwavering stare added to her nervousness. 'You said you needed my help.'

He held out his glass for a refill. After a slight hesitation, she gave it to him. 'In good time,' he said. He settled himself on the couch and put his booted feet on to the coffee table. 'Being here with you is just like old times.'

'Did we ever have old times?'

'We did once. You loved me enough to marry me and have my baby.'

She flinched at the memory. 'I didn't know you then.' She had fallen in love with a man who appeared to be romantic and considerate. It wasn't until after they were married that he turned into a cruel stranger.

'And you think you know me now.' His tone hardened and he tossed back the second sherry before continuing. 'I can assure you, my darling Lee, that you don't. I've let you off lightly until now, giving you the divorce you wanted. Now it's your turn to give me what I want.'

Fear gathered in her body like a tangible thing, spreading tentacles all through her. 'What do you want?'

'Money,' he said flatly. 'I'm in a lot of debt and I'll stay healthier if I can pay it back quickly.'

'You've been gambling again?'

'There's no need to be sanctimonious. We all have our vices.' He looked around the spacious living-room. 'Yours are just different from mine, that's all. I don't sell my body the way it appears you've been doing with the boss of this spread.'

'I work for him, that's all.'

Steve laughed harshly. 'Sure, by day. I was referring to what you do for him after hours.'

She couldn't let him revile Tagg like this. 'You're despicable,' she hissed. 'Get out of this house!'

He picked up the slight hesitation in her voice. 'You nearly said out of *my* house, didn't you?'

'No!'

'Yes, you did. You're forgetting how well I know you, little Lee. But never mind, if you're mistress here—in name or body, it doesn't matter—I can be sure of getting the money I need.'

'How much do you want?'

He named a sum which made her gasp with shock. 'I haven't got anywhere near that much.'

Again, he surveyed the tastefully furnished room. 'Come off it—I know what a set-up like Mundoo must be worth. Millions!'

'But it isn't mine. I can't help you.'

'Yes you can, and you will. The same way you helped me with money when I needed it before.'

She felt the colour drain from her face as she remembered the money he had 'borrowed' from her employer in Sydney. He had helped himself from the petty cash supply when he came to collect her after work one day. She hadn't noticed the loss until she came to balance the accounts. Then Steve had laughed at her when she demanded he replace it. When he refused, she had worked overtime to pay the money back before the loss was discovered. Then there were the other times Steve had tried to force her to obtain money for him. She couldn't go through that again, not even if it meant enduring more of Steve's violence. 'I can't do it,' she whispered.

He sauntered up to her and slid a hand under her chin, forcing her face around to meet his. 'Is it your high principles again, or are you in love with the guy who owns this place?'

Her eyes betrayed her, although she lowered her lashes quickly. 'I ... I'm not.'

He forced her head higher. 'Yes, you are. Does this Laskin character care for you?'

'Yes, he does.'

'Enough to still love you even after he knows about your sordid past?'

Would Tagg still care for her if he knew she had been Steve's accomplice, however unwilling? She would be mortified if Steve managed to tell Tagg what Lee, because she was so frightened he would lose his temper and hurt her or Sally, had been forced to do for him. Steve was very good at covering up his behaviour. No one ever suspected the dark side of his character.

While they were married, people used to tell her how lucky she was to have such a devil-may-care type for a husband. Little did they suspect the violent fiend who lurked underneath his apparently healthy, jokey personality.

'You wouldn't tell him,' she said, half in hope and half in despair.

'You know I would. Come to think of it, telling him may have good results for me. If your grazier won't have you, you'll have no choice but to come back to me, will you?'

He was insane if he thought she'd ever do that. 'I won't be a party to your crimes ever again,' she said levelly. 'I was crazy to think you'd leave me alone if I went along even a little.'

'So you'd rather see me go to gaol—or worse, get beaten up by hoodlums for welching on a debt?'

She paled. 'You're not in debt to—to criminals?'

'What do you think? Never mind, though. When they find my body in an alley somewhere, you'll have to live with the knowledge that you could have helped me and didn't. What will you tell the newspapers when they come to interview you about your ex-husband?'

She was damned no matter what she did. Tagg would never have anything to do with her after that, and Steve was right—she couldn't live with the knowledge that she had been instrumental in his death. 'All right, I'll help you, but I can't give you as much as you need.'

She named a sum which she knew Tagg kept in the cashbox, and to which she had access for the day-to-day running of the property. With luck, she could arrange to go to town tomorrow and obtain a loan for the amount so she could replace it before Tagg returned from his muster.

'It will have to do,' Steve said grudgingly.

She paused at the door. 'But you must promise never to come back here again. This is the last time I'll agree to help you.'

'Sure, sure,' he said a little too readily. 'I'll never darken your doorstep again, promise.'

By now, she knew what Steve's promises were worth, but there was nothing else she could do, so she hurried down the walkway to her office. Tagg's outer door was locked but she had a key to the connecting door between them and she used it to gain access to Tagg's office.

Her heart began to beat faster as she rummaged in the bottom drawer of his filing cabinet for the cashbox she knew was kept there. Praying that it would be full, she carried it to the desk and sat down in Tagg's chair to open it.

When she saw the crisp notes lying there, she faltered, her hand hovering over the box. This was wrong, no matter how Steve justified it! She wouldn't do it, no matter what Steve did to her.

'Help yourself,' said a laconic voice from the doorway.

She looked up to find Tagg framed in the entrance, his key dangling from his fingers.

'I ... er ... I was doing some book-keeping,' she dissembled.

'At this time of night?'

She couldn't lie to him, any more than she could betray her principles and take the money. She shook her head. 'No.'

'Your ex-husband wouldn't be behind this, by any chance?'

In astonishment, she looked up, her face white. 'How did you know?'

'I guessed you were under some sort of pressure from him. I invented the muster so I could keep an eye on you from a distance. And I was right. That bastard came back here demanding money from you, didn't he?'

There was a noise from her office and Steve's voice reached them. 'Come on, Lee, what's taking so long?'

He ground to a halt in the connecting doorway as he saw Tagg waiting there. 'Oh ... uh ... hello. I was ... er ... helping Lee,' he improvised.

Tagg took a menacing step towards him. 'You mean you were helping yourself.'

Steve looked defiantly at Lee. 'It was her idea. She was the one who wanted to give me the money.'

'Then what's stopping her? It's hers to give away, after all.'

Steve looked at Lee in confusion. 'What does he mean, it's yours, Lee?'

Tagg answered for her. 'I mean that everything on this property belongs to Lee. We're engaged to be married.'

CHAPTER SIX

STEVE'S expression was contemptuous. 'So I was right—you are after bigger fish than me! Well, I wish you luck with her, pal. Ask her what kind of treatment she deserves some time.'

Tagg took several menacing steps towards him and Steve backed away. 'One more word, Perry, and so help me, I'll . . .'

'You'll what? Beat me up? I'll slap an assault charge on you so fast you won't know what's hit you,' Steve blustered, although he kept retreating.

'Get out of here,' Tagg said in a low, dangerous voice.

All at once, the fight went out of Steve and he leaned against the door jamb. 'I can't go, not without some money.'

Despite herself, Lee felt sorry for him, pleading so pathetically. 'He's in debt to criminals who will hurt him if we don't help him,' she told Tagg.

He was unmoved. 'Maybe it would teach him a lesson.'

Dispiritedly, Steve began to shuffle out of the office but Tagg halted him with a gesture. 'How much do you need?'

'You mean, you'd give it to me?'

Tagg shook his head. 'No, I mean I'll buy your promise to leave Lee alone from here on. Do I have it?'

'You have it.'

Grimly, Tagg wrote out a cheque and handed the

paper to Steve, holding it by its ends as if it could taint him by association. Steve snatched it away and rushed out with the merest murmur of 'Thanks', almost as if he was afraid Tagg would change his mind and take the money back.

Nothing was said until they heard Steve's car driving away, then Lee turned to Tagg. 'I'll pay you back every cent, I promise.'

'There's no need. I meant what I said, Lee. As my future wife, everything I have is yours for the taking.'

Dumbfounded, she stared at him, feeling her love for him flood over her like a giant tidal wave. 'You can't want to marry me now, after ... after everything that's happened?'

'Nothing's happened to change the way I feel about you. A low animal like Steve Perry would stop at nothing to get what he wanted. I don't blame any woman who gives in to pressure like that.'

'Oh Tagg, I do love you,' she breathed, her voice choked. 'Although I'm not sure I deserve you.'

'Hell, I'm the one who doesn't deserve you,' he said gruffly and moved towards her. 'I often wondered how my Dad managed to fall head over heels for a rancher's daughter he'd only known a few weeks. Now I'm beginning to understand how he felt.' Close now, he looked down at her with those compelling amber eyes which drew her to him like magnets.

'But I'm no heiress,' she murmured, held in thrall by his loving gaze. 'I'm not even much of a catch.'

'Let me be the judge of that,' he instructed and drew her into his arms. This time, she felt only the faintest stirrings of fear and she was able to subdue them in the rapture of being held by him. She swayed as if blown by a phantom wind, and his hold tightened.

She gasped as his lips found the sensitive hollow of her throat. His hand was splayed across her back, arching her to him, while his other hand clasped the firm roundness of her hips, making her vitally aware of his maleness.

The pressure against her tautening stomach muscles told her how badly Tagg wanted her. For the second time in his arms, she knew the powerful onslaught of desire. She wanted him to make love to her.

Keeping her in his arms, he traced kisses along her jawline and forehead, then murmured, 'You haven't given me an answer yet.'

'An answer?'

'Will you marry me? The feeling has to be mutual. Unlike our friend Perry, I don't get my kicks from forcing myself on women.'

'You really do want to marry me?'

He laughed delightedly. 'What does it take to convince you? Yes, in cowboy language, I want you roped and hogtied at my side for the rest of our days.'

'You make me sound like a prize steer,' she teased.

'Well, you are a prize—but a much more precious one, to me, than anything else in the world.'

Was she really hearing this? 'Then yes, I'll marry you,' she consented. 'I love you, Tagg.'

'And I love you, so let's have no more talk of gratitude or kindness. I'm a selfish bastard at heart, and in marrying you I'm really doing myself a favour.'

Worry clouded her bright eyes for a moment. 'Aren't you going to ask me what Steve meant about my previous marriage?' Since Steve had cruelly suggested that he should, the taunt had remained in the air between them.

Tagg's arms tightened around her. 'You'll tell me what you can, when you're ready.'

'And if I'm never ready?'

'Then we'll go on from here.'

She bit her lip. 'There's something you have to know if we're to be married.'

'When,' he said firmly. 'All right, if it will make you feel better.'

This was so difficult. 'I ... we, Steve and I, had a baby, a little girl, Sally. I didn't mean it to happen but I became pregnant almost straight away.' Her voice broke and his arm tightened around her. 'Sally had a congenital liver problem. Only a transplant could have saved her. They ... they didn't find a donor in time.'

'And Sally died.' It wasn't a question. None needed to be asked.

She nodded, overcome with memories. 'She was such a fighter. She hung on until she was two.' Through her tears, she smiled at this particular memory.

'Was Sally the reason you put up with Steve for so long?'

'Yes.' It came out as a whisper. 'We were so short of money I couldn't support her. She needed so much medicine and treatment. Steve said he would hurt her if I ever left him.'

'So you stayed.' He turned her to face him. 'I'm glad you told me, Lee. But that part of your life is over now. Whatever Perry did to you, it's over. He can't hurt you any more unless you let him.'

How she longed for him to be right! Maybe, safe in the knowledge of his love, she could rebuild her

shattered life and learn to love again. Tagg believed it
was possible, therefore she believed it, too.

They returned to the house and opened a bottle of
champagne to toast their engagement. Sipping the
bubbling liquid and staring deep into Tagg's loving
eyes, Lee thought she could never feel more vibrantly
happy than she did now.

Nevertheless, there was another moment which eclipsed
even that one in sheer joy, and that was when Tagg
slipped the wedding ring on to her finger.

They had decided on a civil ceremony in Walgett. Her
parents, happy that she had returned to the conventional
fold at last, flew up for the wedding but had to return to
Orange immediately after the ceremony to look after
Grace's children. Lee's eldest sister was in hospital
expecting her third child, and the beaming grand-
parents were taking care of her family until she was
home with the new baby.

'Won't be long till we're coming up to take care of
your children,' Lee's father told them. Realising what
he had said, her father's eyes darkened. 'I'm sorry, Lee,
I didn't think.'

Tagg's hold on her hand had tightened but she looked
up at him confidently. 'It's all right. They're right to
look to the future instead of the past.'

Tagg put an arm around her shoulders. 'That's
precisely what we intend to do from now on. I just hope
your folks are prepared for the size of brood we plan to
have.'

They hadn't discussed the question of a family but
there was an unspoken agreement between them that
they would both like to. If only Lee could get over the

first hurdle of being able to enjoy a normal marriage.

'You sound as if you're in a hurry to have children,' she said uneasily.

Tagg sensed her worry and squeezed her hand warmly. 'Don't worry, darling, remember my promise?'

He had promised not to make her do anything she didn't want to, she recalled. She hadn't expected him to honour the promise after they were married but she was relieved that he meant to. Her look was filled with loving confidence in him.

'You're very welcome, Mrs Laskin,' he said, reading the look.

Mrs Laskin. How strange it sounded. A few minutes ago she had been Alita Coulthard Perry. Now she was rid of the hated name for ever, and the one which replaced it brought a flush of pride to her cheeks.

Her father gave her a peck on the cheek. 'We'll have to go, love, if we're to be back in Orange in time for Grace's husband to get back to work.'

'Can't you stay for the reception?'

''Fraid not, Lee,' her mother apologised. 'We were lucky to get away for this long.

'Don't look so unhappy,' her father chided. 'We're leaving you in good hands, I can see that.'

Lee leaned forward to accept her mother's kiss. 'My litle girl a grazier's wife!' she crowed. 'You've done us proud, love.'

Tears pricked the backs of Lee's eyes as she walked them to the car and watched them drive off towards the airport. It was silly, at her age, to put so much store by their approval, she realised, but she was childishly pleased anyway. At last she had done something to make them proud of her.

When she said as much to Tagg, he hugged her tightly. 'When we give them grandchildren, they'll be even more pleased,' he promised her.

Her nagging doubts resurfaced. 'Tagg, you didn't marry me just to . . . to give you children, did you?'

His booming laugh brought heads turning their way. 'Good grief, no! Even if we never have kids, I'll still be the proudest man in the district. Hell, there are enough Burnetts in Texas to take care of the future. I just mentioned it because your folks obviously put a lot of store by their grandchildren.'

'They do,' Lee agreed. 'Ever since Grace became a mother, all you hear about is little Brett and little Susan.' They had been proud of Sally, too, and devastated by her loss. They had never spoken about it and Lee wondered if they might blame her for what had happened.

'I'm looking forward to meeting this family of yours,' Tagg was saying. 'Why don't we go to Orange for the christening—if it wouldn't upset you, that is?'

'No, seeing other people's children so happy and well was hard at first, but I've adjusted to it.' She brightened. 'The whole Coulthard clan will be there, and you can meet everyone at once.'

He grinned. 'In that case, I'll have to take you to meet my folks.'

'But they're in Texas!'

'That's right.'

'Oh, Tagg, do you mean it?'

'Why not? You said you'd like to see America. As soon as the shearing is over, we'll go.'

She was brimming with happiness as she watched

Tagg circulate among their wedding guests. He was the tallest and best-looking man in the room, she thought, aware that she was biased but unashamed of the fact.

Most of the wedding guests were returning to Mundoo where Tagg had arranged an outdoor reception. Their neighbours at the various properties were also invited and Lee looked forward to meeting the Beechings of Robina again, as well as Karen's other clients among their neighbours.

Tagg had refused to let her have a hand in planning the reception. He and Mouse had conceived the whole thing in secret, insisting that it be a surprise for her. She couldn't wait to see what they had been up to.

When she saw how they had transformed the home paddock, she gasped with surprise. Yellow ribbons and yellow roses had turned it into a corner of Texas in the western plains of New South Wales. Under an insect-screened marquee, a long trestle table groaned with food, and Tagg informed her proudly that it was all authentic 'down-home' cooking.

He showed her a giant barbecue which held steaks of Mundoo beef wrapped in tortillas, Dallas-style. While the meat was char-broiling, the guests were offered cheese chalupas—a kind of pancake filled with beans and cheese and topped with hot, spicy, avocado sauce.

'Is this what you eat back home?'

'It's barbecue Texas-style,' Tagg informed her. 'I consider this my home but I like to borrow from my other background occasionally just for the fun of it.'

Her smile widened. 'I think I'm going to enjoy having an Aussie cowboy for a husband.'

He leaned across and gently wiped a speck of hot sauce from the corner of her mouth with a napkin, then replaced the food with a light kiss. 'I'm glad you think so.'

'I know so.'

It was too hot for more champagne. The glass Lee had already drunk made her feel light-headed, so she was pleased when Ray di Falco offered her a glass of chilled beer. 'Tagg says it should be Lone Star Beer to be really authentic, but will Foster's do?'

She sipped the cool liquid, feeling it soothe the back of her throat which was on fire from the hot sauce. 'It's fine,' she agreed.

Cheryl, her pregnancy now much more obvious, came up and hugged her. 'I'm so happy for you, Lee. I knew you and the boss were made for each other.'

'It took me longer to be convinced,' Lee told her. 'But I'll never doubt your advice again, honest.'

The two women chatted amicably for a while. Cheryl, as usual, knew everyone and pointed out the various friends and neighbours to Lee, introducing her to those she hadn't yet met.

'Who's the good-looking blonde?' Lee asked, watching Tagg in beated conversation with a tall, coltish-looking woman in skin-tight stonewashed denims and a see-through white blouse.

Cheryl grimaced. 'That's Adora Hamilton from Dingo Crossing. She was the hot favourite to marry Tagg before you came along.'

Lee pretended nonchalance, but her throat muscles constricted as she watched Tagg with his sun-streaked head bent close to the gorgeous blonde one. 'She's very beautiful.'

'And empty-headed,' Cheryl said tartly. She noted Lee's worried expression and let out a breath of

exasperation. 'Don't tell me you're jealous of that flirt!
My lord, you must really be in love.'

'I am.'

Despite Cheryl's assurances that she had nothing to
fear from Adora Hamilton, she was still relieved when
Tagg left the woman and returned to her side. 'Having a
good time?'

'Mmmmm,' she said non-committally.

'But?'

'What makes you think there's a "but"?'

'Your expression.' He looked around, his eyes lighting
on Adora. 'I get it. You were worried about me talking to
an old flame.'

This was more than Cheryl had told her. '*Was* she an
old flame?'

'As a matter of act, yes,' he said evenly. 'But there was
never anything serious in it. Adora hasn't got a serious
thought in her head.'

Lee felt ashamed of her jealousy. 'I'm glad you don't
go for dumb blondes,' she said, making light of it.

He pulled her hard against him so she could feel the
protrusion of his hipbone against her thigh. 'I go for
intense brunettes,' he said firmly, 'and don't you forget
it.' His lips nuzzled her ear and she tried to pull away,
feeling pleasure surge through her like an electric
current.

'Tagg, everyone's watching!'

'Then it's time we went somewhere they can't see us,'
he said, his tone caressing.

In the middle of an answering surge of desire for him,
she felt fear rise like a tide through her. 'B . . . but we're
the hosts, we can't leave.'

'We're also the newly-weds and expected to take off

into the night,' he said.

'Take off where?' Weddings were traditionally followed by honeymoons, of course, but she had assumed, with shearing imminent, that Tagg wouldn't want to take any time off to be alone with her. She realised she had been counting on this to give her time to adjust to her new status.

His next remark dispelled any such hope. 'On our honeymoon, of course. Let's go up to the house and get changed. Ray and Mouse will look after this lot.'

She was acutely conscious of the knowing eyes which followed their progress towards the homestead. One or two people made joking comments and Lee caught a look of pure jealousy from Adora. Even though she had Tagg's assurance that the Hamilton girl meant nothing to him, she felt a shiver of unease.

Learning to trust again was going to be harder than she thought, Lee acknowledged as she walked back to the house. Steve had so eroded her self-confidence that she could hardly imagine any man preferring her to a beauty like Adora Hamilton. But Tagg had left her in no doubt about his loyalties, and despite her fears, Lee lifted her head with pride as she followed Tagg into the house.

Until now, she had remained in her own bedroom, Tagg having accepted that she would prefer to until they were married. Soon she would have to share his room, although the idea of that final commitment provoked a feeling of panic. She fought it down. She loved Tagg and she was going to be a wife to him in every sense. He deserved her faith and she wasn't going to disappoint him or herself.

She didn't hear Tagg come into the room in time to

avert her anxious face from his inspection. 'You're not having second thoughts about me, I hope?' His voice was light but there was an undertone of real concern.

'No, never that.'

'Then get changed and let's go. There's no need to pack. I had Cheryl do it for you while we were in Walgett.'

He must have guessed how reluctant she would be to go away with him, leaving her no excuse to back out. Well, he needn't have worried. She was ready and willing to start their life together. He was right when he said they should look to the future. And that was what she was going to do, starting now.

With new confidence, she slipped out of her lace dress with its tiered layers of petticoats and hung it on a padded hanger. Since she had no idea where Tagg intended to take her, she put on a buttercup-yellow culotte suit Cheryl had talked her into buying just before the wedding. It was pretty enough to be a 'going away' outfit, yet practical in case they had a long way to travel. Aware that Tagg was waiting for her, she hastily repaired her tear-ravaged make-up and went out to join him.

'Pretty as a picture,' he said on seeing her.

The Landcruiser was parked outside, bedecked with the traditional ribbons and old shoes and she climbed into it, feeling self-conscious. She had no idea that Tagg would adhere so closely to tradition. Somehow, she'd thought—or hoped—that they would be married that morning, then come back to Mundoo and go on much as they had before.

Except that nothing was the same any more. She was no longer the hired administrator of the property. She was now Mrs Taggart Laskin, and there was no question of going on as before.

A stream of rice showered over them as the guests clustered around the car. There was a chorus of 'Good luck!' and 'Don't do anything we wouldn't do', and then they were off, leaving the well-wishers behind to continue their party.

'Where are we going?' she asked Tagg.

'You'll soon see—it isn't far.'

The bumpy track which came and went across the paddocks seemed familiar somehow. They were surrounded by the vast, sweeping plains rippling with silver-coloured grass after the recent rains. They passed a brimming waterhole, its blue-green surface rippling in the slight breeze. At the sound of their engine, a great cloud of grey and magenta rose into the air as they disturbed a flock of galahs foraging for insects on the ground.

Occasionally they passed a mob of bleating sheep, gathered nose to tail under the available shade. A few Old Man kangaroos lay on their sides sharing the shade with the sheep. They lifted their heads and watched Tagg's Landcruiser jolt past, their doe-eyes incurious. One or two raised stunted forepaws to scratch themselves, as if emphasising how unimpressed they were with the humans in their noisy vehicle, a speck on the vast unending landscape.

Lee studied it all with a kind of detached interest. Outwardly, she was intent on the passing scene. Inwardly, her fears were returning. Why hadn't she thought that Tagg would want a honeymoon? She could have braced herself for the ordeal instead of allowing herself to be taken by surprise.

She sneaked a sidelong glance at her new husband, taking in the relaxed way his tapering fingers rested on the steering wheel. His spine was straight against the sheepskin seat cover. He looked to be in his element. Lee shook herself. He had promised that she wouldn't be made to do anything she didn't want to do. She would have to start trusting him, and now was a good time.

'Not long now,' he said, smiling at her.

It was an effort to smile back, given the turmoil inside her, but she managed it. 'I'd still like to know where we're going. So far, it looks like the road to Robina.'

'Spot on,' he agreed and slowed the car.

From out of the flat plain emerged the boundary rider's hut in which they had sheltered from the rains. 'We're going to stay here?' she asked. He nodded and helped her out of the car, then escorted her across the paddock to the small timber cabin.

'Our hotel, ma'am.'

Just when she had decided he was out of his mind, he flung open the door and revealed a transformed cabin. The board walls sparkled with fresh white paint; a new rug covered the floorboards and the bed was made up with fresh linen and blankets. 'Like it?'

'You had this done for me?' She was touched.

'I sure did. Remembering how pleasantly we spent the night here the last time, I thought it made a fitting place to start our marriage.'

At the reminder of their altered relationship, she stopped, regarding him uncertainly. The last time they were here, he had no rights over her. But this time . . .

She started to walk into the hut but was forestalled by Tagg. 'Just a minute, Mrs Laskin.'

Before she could ask what was wrong, he scooped her

up in muscular arms. She laughed in spite of her anxiety. 'What are you doing, you crazy Texan?'

'Just carrying you over the threshold, ma'am—a good old Aussie custom, as I recall, so there's no need to be insulting.'

True to his word, he held her until they were inside the cabin then he placed her lightly on her feet. Their eyes met and locked, and Lee swayed towards him instinctively.

Unable to hold back any longer, he grasped her and pulled her against him, resting his lips against her forehead.

'I'm hot and sticky,' she warned him, feeling her heart start to race. Whether it was with fear of what was to come, or with the effect of his nearness, she wasn't sure.

'I don't care, you smell wonderful,' he murmured. 'Like orange blossom.'

'My perfume.' She had chosen it because it reminded her of weddings and today was, after all, her wedding day. She had been too nervous to feel like a bride, but some part of her had wanted to be sentimental.

He breathed deeply. 'That's why I can smell citrus, mixed with ... let's see ... baby powder and ...' he crinkled his nose as he thought, '... you!'

It was impossible to be frightened in the face of his light-hearted teasing. 'I'm glad it's to your liking,' she said pertly, laughter in her voice.

He grew serious. 'Everything about you is to my liking, Lee. That's why I married you.'

'I was wondering about that. You hardly know me. For all you know, Steve could be right about me. Perhaps I don't make a good wife.' It was an admission she had often made to herself. He might as well know the worst now, while there was still time to change his mind.

Firmly, he cupped her chin and tilted her face upwards. 'I'd back my judgement against Steve Perry's any day.' To seal the comment, he dropped a kiss on her parted lips.

It started as a teasing salute but swiftly changed into something deeper. She tasted his mouth, spicy from the hot sauce of the barbecue and slightly sandpapery where his morning shave had begun to wear off. The tiny rasping sensation against her upper lip was utterly erotic and waves of heat suffused her being.

'Mmmmm,' she breathed, hardly aware of having spoken aloud.

'Mmmmm yourself,' he responded, his lips moving sensuously against hers.

His hands slid down her bare arms and he hooked his fingers into the waistband of her culottes, drawing a sharp breath of reaction from her. She was wearing only the tiniest bikini briefs and the skin beneath the top of the culottes was bare, quivering against his fingers.

'God, you're beautiful,' he said and pressed his fingers into her sides so that she drew her stomach muscles in tightly in response.

Then he withdrew his hand, pressed a light kiss on her lips and stepped back a pace.

'What's the matter?' she asked, missing him already although he was only a foot away from her. She wanted him beside her, inside her—she realised with a shock. He had aroused her to such a pitch that she had forgotten to be frightened.

'Nothing,' he said hoarsely. 'I just remembered that all our supplies are still out in the car.'

'Don't go, don't leave me,' she wanted to cry out. 'It's all right, I can handle it.'

But some deep-seated reservation stilled her tongue. What if she provoked him beyond endurance and then she was unable to go through with their lovemaking? It wouldn't be fair to Tagg. All the same, she half wished he would stop being so considerate and take her there and then while she was still quivering with desire for him.

She had never felt this way with Steve, she thought as she watched Tagg unload the car through the window. He had never cared how she felt, or even asked her whether she felt anything at all. The only time he had been responsive to her feelings was when she cried out in pain, or tried to escape his fury. Then he became even more violent, despising her for her fear.

Screwing up her eyes to shut out the memory, she leaned against the wooden table, now mended and painted so it looked new. She was so confused. One minute, she was on fire for Tagg and the next, she was remembering the last few times with Steve.

'It won't be like that. It will be different,' she told herself over and over. For both their sakes, she had to believe it.

CHAPTER SEVEN

WHEN Tagg kicked the door open with his foot, Lee took the box of provisions from him and placed it on the table. 'You've brought a whole store with you,' she said, looking at the variety of goodies. A jar of red caviar sat atop a long crusty loaf, and the neck of a bottle of champagne protruded from under that.

'Since we don't have refrigeration here, I had to bring food which would travel well,' he explained.

She giggled. 'Well, at least I know now that caviar and champagne travel well.'

He clasped her around the waist and swung her into the air. 'This is our day. I thought we should celebrate in style.'

When her feet touched the ground again, she stepped out of the circle of his arms and began unpacking the supplies, putting them on the wooden shelf which spanned one wall.

After a few minutes watching her at work, he took the jar of caviar from her hand, set it on the shelf and closed the box. 'We can do that later.'

Oh God, he wasn't going to honour his promise after all! His eyes on her were warm, the desire in them unmistakable. He wanted to make love to her and she just wasn't ready. Frantically, she looked around the small room. 'I ... er ... where's the bathroom?' she asked.

His answering smile was wry, telling her plainly that he knew she was playing for time. 'There isn't one. The

117

toilet—or, as they say here, the dinkum dunny—is around the back. I had it cleaned and checked for spiders and snakes, so you need have no fear of using it. And as for bathing—there's a creek at the bottom of this paddock.'

Without looking at him, she fled from the room. But she didn't go to the small building behind the cabin. Instead, she walked across the paddock to where Tagg had indicated she would find the creek.

She was running away again, and both of them knew it. But she just couldn't seem to stop herself.

It was a long walk from the cabin to the creek, which turned out to be a winding ribbon of water, set in a deep cleft of eroded soil. Reaching it, she stopped to look around, letting the beauty and peace of the place envelop her.

The creek looked innocent, deceptively so, she thought, remembering how swiftly such trickles had turned into raging torrents in the rain. The exposed roots of the river red gums and coolibah trees testified to the power of the water in full flood.

Leaning against one of the gaunt gum trees, its bark scribbled with insect trails, she took slow, deep breaths to calm herself. Sooner or later she would have to go back and fulfil her obligations as Tagg's wife. But not yet, it was too soon.

Refusing to consider the problem any longer, her mind began registering the myriad details of the bush around her.

In the dusky silence, the bush came to life. Grey kangaroos peeped from behind the trees and went on feeding, unconcerned by her presence. Overhead, a flock of sulphur-crested cockatoos wheeled and screeched their raucous cries. And on the ground across the paddocks, dozens of Red-Rumped parrots—in fact, a lovely jewelled sea-green—chattered as they grubbed for insects.

How she loved the bush—and Mundoo Run. And its formidable boss? she asked herself. Yes, she loved him. He was the most caring and considerate man she had ever met. He shared her love of the land and of beauty for its own sake. They belonged together.

So why was she mooning around beside a creek when he was waiting for her? With ever-quickening steps, she began to walk back to the cabin.

When she got there, Tagg had moved the wooden table to the grass outside, covering it with a chequered cloth. On it, he had set out the champagne, two glasses, and plates of caviar, crusty bread, and halves of succulent melon. He smiled as she approached, and pulled out one of the rickety chairs for her.

'You didn't tell me we were dining *al fresco*,' she said, catching some of his playful mood.

'Not only that, but outdoors as well,' he rejoined, winking at her. He poured champagne into their glasses and lifted his. 'To my lovely new bride.'

She returned the gesture, sipping the champagne then setting the glass down again. 'Tagg—why did you marry me?'

'Because I fell in love with you,' he affirmed.

'Yes, but why did you fall in love with me?'

'Ah, the lady is fishing for compliments!'

'No, I'm not. I was wondering, that's all.'

He grew more serious. 'You're wondering whether it will last, aren't you? Well, only time can tell us that. It didn't for you with your first husband. And it didn't for my father. Maybe it won't for us—but I intend to give it the old college try, believe me.'

'You still haven't answered my question,' she insisted. It had suddenly become vital for her to know just what he saw in her. She knew what she saw in him, but still found it hard to believe that such a man could really love her for herself. There had to be some other reason, something she hadn't thought of yet. 'It wasn't charity, was it?' she asked.

He laughed loudly and the sound echoed around the paddocks. 'Good God, no! Taking you to bed and making passionate love to you to cure you of your hang-ups—now *that* would have been an act of charity. Marrying you was for more selfish reasons.'

'Such as?'

He played with the stem of his champagne glass, staring deep into the bubbling liquid. 'I wanted to sleep with you. I can't deny that. But sex wasn't the only reason. I guess I want a partner who shares every facet of my life. I'm committed to Mundoo, you know that, so you had to love the place as much as I do. And you had to put up with my foibles, like the hours I spend in my lab trying to breed new strains of grass to drought-proof the station.'

'I thought that was a serious pursuit, not a foible,' she said readily.

His dark eyes sparkled and the corners of his mouth turned upwards. 'Now that's one of the things I love about you. You take my work seriously—not like the fluffy-headed Miss Hamilton, who refers to my tissue cultures as my test-tube babies.'

Lee laughed in spite of herself. 'She actually called them that?'

He held up his hand. 'Her words exactly, I swear.' He began ticking off points on his fingers. 'So you love my home and my work—that's two strikes for you. You're beautiful and unselfish, which is a rare combination. I *think* you love me.' His look contained a trace of uncertainty.

She was quick to reassure him. 'I do, Tagg. Have no fears about that. I may not be very good at showing you, but I've loved you from our first meeting.'

'Then there's another reason which is important to me.'

'Which is?'

He took her hand, curling the fingers into his palm so that her whole hand was enclosed in his. 'You and I both want a lasting relationship. I know we can't guarantee it, but I could never marry a woman who thought she could always get a divorce if it didn't work out.'

Was he telling her that he wouldn't let her go even if she was unable to consummate their marriage? It certainly sounded that way. 'I want marriage to be for keeps,' she said uncertainly.

'And so do I. I don't believe in staying together at any price, not if things aren't right between you. But I abhor the modern habit of treating a relationship as if it was disposable, something you buy, try and throw away.' He leaned forward. 'You know, I almost married an American girl once. Grandpa Burnett engineered it, I found out later. He thought it would keep me in Texas. I really believed I loved her and she loved me.'

'What went wrong?'

His hold on her fingers tightened. 'She wanted me to sign a pre-marital agreement setting out how our properties were to be divided in the event of a divorce.'

'I see what you mean.' Even though she had a failed marriage behind her, Lee couldn't envisage starting off on such a negative note, no matter how sensible it might be. 'I guess we're both old-fashioned about marriage,' she conceded. 'I was brought up to believe it was a for ever thing, too.'

'It was the opposite for me,' he explained. 'Seeing the misery my folks went through, and knowing how it felt to be caught in the middle, I would never put a child through that unless there was no other solution.'

She capped his hand with her free one. 'It must have been terrible for you.'

'It was,' he said shortly. 'But let's not talk about the past. Today is the first day of the rest of our lives, as they say. Let's drink to the future.'

This time, Lee willingly joined him in the toast, and drained her glass enthusiastically. The elated feeling which came with the wine gave her an idea. If she drank enough, she might summon the courage to let Tagg make love to her. God knew, she wanted him, too. She just couldn't make her body co-operate. Perhaps after a few drinks, she would stop fighting him.

After she had finished her second glass and held it out for a refill, he took it from her. 'Are you really so scared of spending the night with me that you have to be drunk to get through it?'

Miserably, she nodded. 'It isn't your fault, Tagg . . . I meant it when I said I love you. It's just . . .'

'The willing spirit and the weak flesh,' he guessed. 'Don't look so frightened. I promised not to do anything you didn't want me to, and I meant it.'

Her relief was almost palpable. 'Even now?'

'Even now.' He stood up. 'We'd better stow the food away or the possums will have a midnight feast. But the rest of the clearing up can wait until morning.'

While they dined, night had fallen and the moon cast a silver glow over the landscape, transforming it into a fairyland of ghostly trees and shivery silver grasses. The night was filled with the rustling sounds of nocturnal animals and the air throbbed with the beat of wings and the soft whoosh of gliding possums as they spread their cape-like skins and soared from tree to tree. Night-feeding kangaroos and wallabies thumped the ground as they bounded through the undergrowth and small ground animals scuttled away with rustling sounds.

It was a living, breathing landscape. Never before had Lee been so conscious that she was part of it. For a long time, she stood outside the cabin, savouring the experience. She wasn't afraid to go inside, she told herself. The night was beautiful and vibrant and she hated shutting it out.

Yet she was shutting Tagg out, she told herself. He didn't deserve to be treated this way. She felt ashamed of her earlier impulse to get drunk enough to let him make love to her, and was glad he had seen through her attempt.

Behind her, the door creaked open. 'Come to bed, Lee,' he commanded softly.

Since there was nothing else she could do, she turned and followed him into the cabin.

In contrast to the last time they had slept here, the bed looked fresh and inviting with its new mattress and coverings. Tagg had lit the kerosene lamp which hissed softly on the table, and cast a soft yellow glow over everything.

He was already lying in bed, his torso naked as he lay propped up on one elbow against the wall. Last time, he had averted his eyes while she changed. This time, he watched her appreciatively as she slowly lifted the yellow top over her head.

'You have a lovely body, Lee,' he said huskily.

As if in a dream, she slid the culottes off so that she

stood before him in pale lilac bikini briefs and matching bra. Her breasts rose and fell rhythmically, in time with her laboured breathing.

She looked around. 'Where's my nightdress?' Surely Cheryl had remembered to pack some for her?

'You won't need it. The night is warm.'

All the same, she turned out the lamp so the cabin was illuminated only by moonlight, before she removed her underwear. Unable to put off the moment any longer, she padded towards the bed where Tagg had turned back the covers invitingly.

As soon as she lay down beside him, the backs of her legs contacted his smooth stomach and thighs, and she discovered with a shock that he wasn't wearing anything either. She withdrew to the far edge of the bed, putting as much distance as possible between them.

He let her lie like that for a few minutes, then hooked an arm over her hips. 'You can't be comfortable like that.'

The contact sent a jolt like electricity through her. Her breathing became fast and shallow. It took every ounce of her courage not to leap out of the bed. 'I am, honestly.'

'When someone says "honestly", it's usually anything but the truth,' he chided her.

Reluctantly, she rolled over on to her back and tucked an arm behind her head. 'All right, is that better?'

'Much better.' There was a long pause. 'Would it frighten you too much if I kissed you?'

'No.'

The answer caught her by surprise and she realised it was true. The feel of his body against her side was awakening within her sensations she didn't want to acknowledge, but couldn't ignore, either.

He lifted himself on to one arm and leaned across her, his curling chest hairs teasing her skin. In the moonlight, his face seemed to be carved from granite, the planes and hollows shadowed and forbidding. But when his mouth found hers, there was nothing statue-like about his kiss.

At first his touch was feather-light, then he increased the pressure until she felt as if a flame had been ignited inside her. Her response was instinctive.

Only when she felt his touch become more urgent, a little harder, more dominant, did she feel suddenly threatened, and she pushed him away with frantic hands. The similarity between the insistence of Tagg's touch and the angry strength of Steve's made the memories flood back, chilling the blood with unreason-able but ungovernable panic. 'Don't, please ...'

At once, he lay down on his side of the bed, although the hard edge of his thigh was still in touch with hers.

Now he was angry and disappointed, as he had every right to be. 'I'm sorry, Tagg,' she said miserably.

'Don't apologise. I knew it would take time,' he said gently.

His compassion brought tears to her eyes. 'Then you don't mind?'

'I wouldn't be human if I said that. But I love you and I don't want to hurt you.'

'I don't want to hurt you, either,' she agreed. 'So what do we do now?'

'Simple,' he said. 'If you can't let me make love to you—you make love to me.'

Throughout her marriage, Steve had never encour-aged her to take the initiative. She had always felt that he preferred a position of power in bed, as he did out of it. She sat up and looked at Tagg uncertainly, not sure what he expected her to do next.

He sensed her indecision. 'Just do whatever your instincts tell you to,' he instructed. 'Don't be afraid to touch me, I shan't break.'

The idea of his rock-hard body being fragile made her laugh and broke the tension spell. Tentatively, she reached out a hand and stroked his chest above the covers. In the dark, her fingers were more sensitive and the feel of his firm yet yielding skin, thinly strewn with hair, was exciting.

When he remained passive under her hands, she gained the confidence to venture lower, massaging his skin with increasingly firm strokes. Only his laboured breathing betrayed how her touch was affecting him.

She encountered the nobby protrusion of his hipbones under skin as firm yet elastic as the head of a drum. His stomach was flat and his chest hair tapered to a V, before blossoming out into a thick mat, she found as she continued her explorations.

When her fingers curled into the mat, he drew a sharp breath and she knew he couldn't wait for her much longer. She reached a decision. Whatever he did to her, it would be all right. They loved each other and that was what mattered. He wouldn't hurt her. She had to believe that.

'Love me, Tagg,' she whispered.

'Are you sure?'

'I'm sure.'

With a groan, he rolled over and took her in his arms, moulding their bodies together. Only then did she realise what limits of endurance she had taken him to. Even so, he made sure she was ready for him, before he claimed her fully.

This couldn't be lovemaking, this rapturous joining

of two bodies and souls, she thought wildly as her excitement mounted to fever pitch. She had never known such ecstasy existed. Yet there was even greater joy in store as Tagg coaxed her to ever-dizzier heights of pleasure. She was one with the wedge-tail eagles, soaring high on unseen currents, spreading her wings in joyous communion with the elements.

Afterwards, they lay easily side by side. She could tell that Tagg was still awake by the shallowness of his breathing. 'I didn't know it could be like this,' she said into the darkness.

'It can always be like this for us,' he assured her. 'If you're willing to trust me.'

'Always,' she murmured, and her hand slid into his under the covers.

Next morning she awoke with the feeling that something was gloriously, wonderfully right. When she turned her head and saw Tagg's dark one resting on the pillow she remembered what it was. She had become his wife yesterday, in name and in fact. No longer need she be afraid of disappointing him.

As she watched him, he opened his eyes and smiled back. 'Good morning, Mrs Laskin.'

How good it sounded! 'Good morning, Mr Laskin,' she answered smiling back.

'You looked very thoughtful just now. What were you thinking about?' he asked.

Her heightened colour should have told him, but she couldn't find the words so she said, 'I was wondering what we're going to do today.'

His smile broadened and he slid an arm across her stomach. 'I can think of something,' he volunteered, his eyes growing warm.

Last night, his comment would have started another

panic attack, but this morning she was a different person—made whole by Tagg's love and understanding. She rolled over and linked her arms around his neck so their mouths were on a level. 'I can't imagine what it could be.'

He proceeded to show her with, if possible, more ecstatic effect than last night. This time, she had no reservations about giving herself to him, and her willing responses delighted him.

'My, you are a fast learner,' he told her.

Her love for him was transparent in her eyes. 'I had the best teacher.'

It was some time later before they ventured out of the cabin and breakfasted on fresh fruit, cheese and damper in the shade of a coolibah tree. Lee thought she had never been so happy.

After that, they strolled down to the creek which looked cool and inviting in the shimmering morning heat. 'Feel like a swim?' Tagg asked. 'It's quite safe here. The bottom is sandy.'

She shook her head. 'I don't think Cheryl packed a swimsuit for me.'

He laughed. 'She didn't pack one for me either, so we're even.'

'I've never been skinny dipping before.'

'There's a first time for everything.'

Suiting the action to the word, he skimmed his shirt off over his head, revealing a broad expanse of tanned chest which gleamed like burnished timber in the sunlight. When he reached for the zipper of his jeans, she looked away.

'You weren't so shy last night,' he reminded her.

'That was different. It was dark and . . .' She tailed off. How could she explain the sudden sensation of arousal which assailed her as he undressed? He thought she was overcome with shyness. What would he say if he knew it was almost the opposite? God, how she had changed in the short space of time since last night!

At the same time, another thought cast a shadow over her happiness. How long could this idyll last? Sooner or later Tagg would want to know the truth about her marriage to Steve, then the lovelight in his eyes would be replaced by pity or contempt. She couldn't bear it if that happened.

While she had been standing in indecision, Tagg had finished undressing and was now luxuriating in the cool water. 'Come on in, it's glorious,' he urged.

He struck out for the far bank and she used the opportunity to strip off her shirt and jeans, and plunge in. Tagg was right. The water felt like velvet against her sun-warmed skin.

As she floated in the shallows, enjoying the feeling, he swam up behind her and caught her around the middle, sweeping her into his arms. The feel of their wet flesh entwined sent surges of desire all through her being.

'Happy?' he asked, kissing her.

'Unbelievably happy,' she responded, then gave herself up to the joy of being in his arms.

They made love again on the riverbank, in the shade of the red gums. Tagg spread his shirt out as a blanket for them and lowered her on to it. When she protested that the shirt would get wet, he dismissed it, saying it was warm enough to dry anything.

At lunchtime, Tagg caught a freshwater catfish which he barbecued on the riverbank. They ate with their fingers, washing the fish down with more of the champagne they had brought with them.

Eden must have been like this, Lee thought wonderingly, drinking in the dear sight of Tagg stretched out on the bank, sleeping off his lunch. He looked like a dreamtime spirit as he lay on his back with one arm flung over his eyes.

She should have remembered what happened to the inhabitants of Eden . . .

As they walked back towards the cabin that afternoon, Tagg took her hand and urged her in a new direction.

'Where are you taking me?' she asked, laughing.

'I have something to show you,' was all he would tell her.

They walked for some time across the paddocks until they arrived at a stand of ancient eucalyptus trees, standing gaunt and bare of leaves, like a collection of pitchforks speared into the ground, their tines reaching for the sky.

'What is this place?'

'One of my boyhood haunts,' he confessed. 'I wanted you to see it, don't ask me why. I guess I want you to know all my secrets.'

She felt a twinge of unease as he showed her this place where he had played as a young boy, before he was taken back to America. He wanted to share all his secrets with her. How long would it be before he demanded the same from her?

In the centre of the grove was a weird old eucalyptus, growing in an S-shape. Cut deep into the bark, and long overgrown, were the letters 'TL loves AH'. 'Adora Hamilton?' Lee guessed.

Tagg nodded. 'In those days she was a skinny eight-year-old tomboy with her hair in pigtails. Her father owned the most amazing chestnut gelding and I courted Adora so she'd let me ride it in the picnic races. She made me take her to a costume party in payment.' His grimace told her what he thought of such activities.

'It sounds like a very practical courtship,' Lee observed. All the same, she wondered what would have come of the childish courtship if Tagg hadn't been taken away. She dismissed the thought as unworthy. Tagg had made it perfectly clear that she had nothing to fear from Adora Hamilton. Surely his willingness to show her this evidence of his past infatuation proved it?

Nevertheless, her uneasiness persisted. She knew what caused it. Everything was just too perfect. Tagg loved her. She had proved she was able to respond to his love. Something was bound to come along and burst the bubble.

It happened as they were walking back towards the cabin. On the skyline, Tagg noticed a horseman riding towards them. 'It's Bill Drury, one of the stockmen,' he said.

The man caught up with them outside the cabin, and slid off his horse, dropping the reins over the animal's head. 'G'day, boss, Mrs Laskin,' he said, touching his hat to her.

'What's up, Bill?' Tagg asked, his tone anxious.

'Nothing yet, boss, but Ray is worried that there might be. He asked me to send you his apologies and ask whether you'd mind coming back to the homestead tonight instead of tomorrow.'

Lee and Tagg exchanged worried glances; Ray wasn't the type to interrupt their short honeymoon unless he had a real problem. 'Did he say what was the matter?' she asked.

The stockman addressed his reply to Tagg. 'It's his missus, boss. She's having a bit of trouble with the baby. They've phoned the doctor and taken his advice, but Ray's worried they might have to go into town at short notice and he'd like you to be on hand just in case.'

Tagg's response was immediate. 'No problem. You head back. We'll load up the car and be right behind you.'

After Bill Drury mounted up again and rode off, they went into the cabin and started loading their supplies in anxious silence. When they were on the road again, Tagg turned to her. 'I hope you aren't too upset about having your honeymoon interrupted.'

'It's your honeymoon, too, and I'd much rather be there to help Cheryl in case she needs us.'

His appreciative smile told her he was glad she wasn't making a fuss. In a way, she was relieved to be returning to Mundoo. As long as they were camped out here in the wilderness, bathing in the creek and picknicking on fruit and fish, she felt as if she was dreaming. Only when she was back at Mundoo would she start to believe her marriage was real.

They made it back in record time and Lee went straight to the manager's cottage to check on Cheryl, while Tagg took their things into the main house and consulted with Ray.

Cheryl's answering call was weak when Lee knocked on the door and she went straight in. Cheryl lay on her bed and looked pale and ill, unlike her usual cheerful self. 'How are you feeling?' Lee asked.

'Terrible, but I'm glad you've come.' She grasped Lee's hand. 'Oh God, Lee, I don't want anything to happen to this baby.'

'Nothing's going to,' Lee assured her, wondering at the same time if it was true. She couldn't help remembering the terror she had felt when her own baby's life was in jeopardy. She fought the memory. Cheryl needed her now. 'What did the doctor say?' she asked, keeping her voice neutral.

'He ordered me straight to bed for complete rest. He called in himself an hour ago and he didn't seem too worried, but he said if I have any more trouble I'll have to go straight to hospital.'

'Then it can't be too bad, or he would have stayed around.'

Cheryl grimaced. 'He didn't want to leave, but one of the men over at Dingo Crossing fell under a tractor, so he had no choice.'

Life was so hard in the bush, Lee thought. Help was so far away. it was a grim fact to face, but one which every man, woman and child of the bush accepted.

She stayed with Cheryl until the other woman started to doze, then she let herself out quietly and hurried across the garden to the main house. Maybe Ray could tell her more about what the doctor had said.

Voices emanated from the office, telling her Ray and Tagg were there, and she joined them. She was unprepared for the grim look of accusation Tagg directed at her as she walked in. 'What's the matter?' she asked, looking uncertainly at Ray and back to Tagg.

He thrust a cheque book across the desk to her. 'This is the matter.'

She looked at the stub in front of her and felt the colour leave her face. It was made out to Steven Perry for a considerable sum in cash, and carried yesterday's date. 'Steve was here?' she whispered, although the fact was obvious.

'And you didn't know a thing about it?'

Why did he sound so accusing? 'No, I didn't. I thought he'd gone for good after you paid his debts the last time.'

Tagg ran a hand through his hair. 'Well, you thought

wrong. He turned up here and told Ray I had arranged to pay him another cheque.'

Ray nodded unhappily. 'I wasn't sure what to do, what with worrying about Cheryl and all, but he was so confident about it. He said the boss had already paid him half of what he was owed, and I was to pay him the balance. I looked in the cheque book and sure enough, there was the previous cheque. He offered to wait until you got back, and that clinched it for me. I thought he must be on the up-and-up.'

What a shrewd operator Steve was, she thought bitterly. He had known about the wedding, and had timed his visit to the minute. Even his offer to wait for their return was calculated to inspire Ray's confidence.

She sank down into a visitor's chair. 'I swear I didn't know anything about this,' she said.

'I know, and I'm sorry I sounded off at you,' Tagg apologised. 'But this guy just doesn't know when to quit.' He reached for the telephone.

'What are you going to do?'

'Call the local police and have him arrested for fraud.'

If he did that, there would be publicity in the local papers and Steve would almost certainly make good his threat to tell everyone about Alita's past. How could she stay here as Tagg's wife after that? 'Oh, please don't,' she begged. 'Can't you just forget about it? He's probably long gone by now.'

Slowly, Tagg replaced the receiver, and looked at Ray. 'Would you give us a few minutes alone, Ray?'

The manager left, obviously anxious to get back to his wife. Then Tagg leaned across the desk, his eyes hard. 'Now, would you tell me why you want me to treat your ex-husband with kid gloves?' Before she could answer, he supplied his own. 'It's because you still care for him, isn't it? Oh, my God, you're still in love with him!'

No! You've got it all wrong, she wanted to scream, but she couldn't speak for the tears choking her throat. She had no choice, she would have to tell him the whole sordid story right now, if she was to convince him he was wrong about her and Steve.

But before she could speak, they were interrupted by a distraught Ray who burst into the office again. He shot a brief look of apology at Lee, then turned to Tagg. 'Sorry about this, boss, but I've got to get Cheryl to hospital. I think she's going to lose the baby.'

CHAPTER EIGHT

CHERYL's eyes fluttered open and her fingers plucked at the bedlinen. 'Is the baby all right?'

'Yes, darling, rest now. Everything's going to be fine.'

Watching Ray bending over his wife brought a lump to Lee's throat. Quietly, she slipped out of the room and left them alone. Outside in the waiting room, she helped herself to coffee from a dispenser and sat down to wait for Ray to take her to a hotel as they'd agreed. She was to stay in town until Cheryl was fully recovered.

After that ... she wasn't sure. Tagg's accusing expression still haunted her. How could he think that she could still feel anything for Steve? If she did, surely she wouldn't have married Tagg, couldn't he see that? Apparently not. She wondered if he really knew her at all.

Ray's interruption had come just as she was about to tell Tagg about her marriage to Steve. But her own concerns had been swept aside and she had volunteered to travel to the hospital with Cheryl. Her honeymoon luggage still stood on the veranda, and she snatched it up and carried it to Ray's waiting car. He gave her a grateful look. 'I'm glad you're coming along. You can keep Cheryl calm while I concentrate on the driving.'

'What about young Craigie?' she asked.

'I've asked Mrs Drury to look after him at her cottage until we get back,' he explained. 'Bill is going to radio

Dingo Crossing and ask the doctor to meet us at the hospital.'

Marvelling at his efficiency when he must be out of his mind with worry, Lee returned to the di Falcos' cottage and packed some clothes for Cheryl.

'I feel such an idiot, causing all this fuss,' Cheryl said as she watched from the bed.

Lee forced herself to sound cheerful. 'Look at it this way, you're giving the others something to gossip about for a change.'

The trip to town had been a nightmare, with Cheryl having to be kept calm and still, not an easy task on the bumpy road. Somehow they had managed it, and the doctor assured them the baby was all right, although it had been close.

'She should stay here for a few days as a precaution,' he told them.

Ray's leathery brow crinkled. 'Gee, doctor, I can't stay here for very long. We've got another little lad at home and he'll be pining for us.'

Lee didn't hesitate. 'I'll stay here with Cheryl, Ray. There's no reason for me to hurry back to Mundoo. I'm all caught up with the paperwork.'

'Are you sure? You were on your honeymoon, after all.'

She'd all but forgotten the fact. 'I don't think Tagg will mind,' she said truthfully.

Ray grinned. 'In his shoes, I'd mind like hell. But it would mean a lot to me 'n' Cheryl to have you here.'

'Then it's settled. I'll stay.'

In a way, the decision was like a reprieve. For a few more days, she had a legitimate reason to postpone her talk with Tagg. She wasn't looking forward to telling him about her marriage to Steve. But there was no other way if he was ever to trust her again.

When she rang Tagg to tell him that she was remaining in Walgett for a while, he was cool and distant. His enquiries about Cheryl and the baby were warm enough, but when she asked whether he minded her staying away, his tone changed. 'Might be a good idea at that,' he said. 'Give us both a chance to think things over.'

Fear stabbed through her like a knife. Think what over? Was he regretting their marriage to the extent that he wanted to end it? He had said he wanted their marriage to last, yet he was ready to jeopardise it with suspicion. She couldn't bring herself to ask him what he planned to do, fearing the answer. Instead, she said, 'I love you, Tagg,' and hung up before he could respond.

Footsteps further down the corridor told her Ray was coming, and Lee stood up.

He smiled when he saw her. 'Ready to go?'

'Yes. Is Cheryl all right?'

'She's resting now. It's the best thing she can do, the doc says.' He held up a thumb and forefinger an inch apart. 'She came that close to losing the baby. If we hadn't got her here in time . . .' His voice broke.

'But we made it, didn't we?' Lee said brightly, taking his arm.

He clasped a hand over hers. 'I don't know what we'd have done without you, lass. Now I know what the boss sees in you. You have a real heart, no mistake.'

He didn't know what else the boss saw in her, she thought ruefully. Tagg had made it clear that he blamed her for Steve's continual hanging around—thought that she hadn't been able to tell him to leave her alone, because she still cared for him. If only she had told Tagg the whole story when Steve first came to Mundoo, then none of this would have happened! Lee knew better than anyone how Steve's devious mind worked. The first cheque had only given him the idea that there might be more where that came from.

She sighed heavily. Was she never to be rid of his evil influence in her life?

'Tired, lass?' Ray asked in concern.

'No, I was thinking about the money Steve conned you into giving him,' she confessed.

Ray muttered under his breath. 'I'd like to get my hands on that crook! I really fell for his line about Tagg owing him the money.'

She hadn't intended to make Ray feel worse than he did already. 'It wasn't your fault,' she assured him. 'You had a lot on your mind. Besides, Steve Perry has duped a lot of people.' Me most of all, she added to herself.

'All the same, if I ever get hold of him . . .' He left the threat unspoken.

They pulled up outside a hotel and Lee saw with a jolt that it was the one where she and Tagg had spent their first night together. Ray had chosen it without consulting her. She was tempted to ask him to take her somewhere else but it would look strange without an explanation—and what could she tell him—that she was afraid of a few memories?

By an unkind coincidence, she was allocated the same room she had occupied before. As she stood inside it, she had a strong sensation of Tagg, standing in the doorway and she blinked rapidly. She was behaving like a lovesick fool. Their marriage wasn't over yet. Lots of couples experienced rough patches at the start.

Except that this wasn't a rough patch—it was much worse. Tagg believed she had married him so Steve could gain access to his money. Since she hadn't given him any reason to believe otherwise, she could see where he got this idea.

He probably thought her fears were part of the same act, she realised miserably. Was he regretting being so kind and patient with her? She was tempted to telephone him right away but the thought of his cold response when she had called earlier deterred her. What if he refused to listen to her explanations and instead, told her not to bother coming back?

Tormented by such thoughts, she refused Ray's offer of dinner. 'I'll buy a sandwich and have it in my room,' she told him. 'It's been a long day.'

He nodded in understanding. 'In that case, I'll get something at the hospital when I go to see Cheryl this evening during visiting hours.'

'Give her my love and tell her I'll see her tomorrow,' she asked.

'I will. She'll be so glad you're staying in town. She won't feel so lonely after I go back to Mundoo tomorrow.'

Cheryl echoed her husband's sentiments when Lee arrived at the hospital the following day. 'Are you sure the boss can spare his new wife?' she asked.

'A couple of days won't hurt him,' Lee said, forcing a laugh.

Cheryl frowned. 'There's nothing wrong between you two, is there?'

'Of course not. Stop looking so worried. The doctor said you had to stay calm.'

'It's difficult, but I'll try.' She gestured around the

hospital room where flowers from Ray and her friends at Mundoo were banked high. 'I'd never forgive myself if I came between you two, that's all.'

Horrified, Lee realised that Cheryl was blaming herself for the interrupted honeymoon. She grasped the other woman's hand. 'Nothing's wrong, so put it out of your mind,' she said firmly. 'You couldn't help what happened. I'm just glad I was able to help.'

They talked for a little longer, with Lee carefully steering the conversation away from herself and Tagg. She was relieved when the nurse reminded them that visiting hours were over. 'I'll come and see you tomorrow,' she promised as she stood up to leave.

Outside in the spring sunshine once more, Lee hesitated. The day stretched ahead of her and the idea of returning to her lonely hotel room wasn't appealing. She decided to treat herself to lunch in one of the attractive cafés the town offered.

As she strolled along, glancing idly in the shop windows, she was surprised to hear footsteps hurrying up behind her. 'Lee, wait!'

'Karen!' She whirled around to find her friend rushing up with arms outstretched. The two girls hugged one another, both talking at once. Finally, Lee was able to step back a little. 'What are you doing here?'

'I live here, remember? Kevin and I got home from Fiji yesterday. I went straight to Mundoo to see you, and Tagg told me what had happened. Poor Cheryl!'

So he hadn't told Karen everything. 'Yes, it was touch and go for a while but the baby's OK—they both are,' she supplied.

At Karen's insistence, they went to a nearby café and sat at a window table where they could watch the passing parade as they caught up on each other's news.

After ordering omelettes and fruit juice, they sat suddenly tongue-tied, then both spoke at once.

'How have you . . .?'

'Tell me, did you . . .?'

Karen laughed. 'You first.'

Where on earth did she start? 'I've been looking after your business fairly well—at least none of your clients has cancelled the service.'

Gesturing impatiently, Karen leaned across the table. 'I know all that. I want to hear about you and Tagg Laskin.' She grasped Lee's left hand which now sported a wide gold wedding band. 'This, for instance.'

'You mean you already know?'

'This is a small town. News travels fast. I was just enjoying the suspense.' She winked slyly. 'It's one way to keep a client, I suppose.' Then she squeezed Lee's hand. 'I'm only joking. I'm very happy for you. Tagg's a great guy.'

Lee ducked her head. 'I know.'

'But?'

Karen knew her too well for pretence. 'But it isn't working out.'

She went on to tell Karen about Steve's reappearance. When she described how he had taken advantage of Tagg's absence to con Ray out of more money, Karen whistled softly. 'I know Steve said he would get back at you for leaving him, but I never dreamed he'd go this far.'

'I should have guessed,' Lee said miserably. 'The only rules Steve lives by are his own.'

'What will you do now? You can't just give up on Tagg, not when it's obvious you love him so much.'

'I'm afraid he's given up on me.'

Karen clucked her tongue impatiently. 'You don't get it, do you?' Lee shook her head. 'The reason Tagg was so upset about all this is because it smacks of the way his mother conned his father into marrying her. You've heard the story?'

'Yes, he told me. And now he thinks I'm as bad as her.' She couldn't blame him. So far she hadn't given Tagg any reason to trust her—the opposite in fact. By apparently defending Steve, she had fuelled Tagg's suspicion that she was in league with him.

They were interrupted while the waitress served their lunch, which they ate in silence for a while. Then Lee said, 'That's enough about me. Tell me about your honeymoon.'

Karen's eyes shone as she described her stay on Fiji's Coral Coast. She and Kevin had taken part in a fish drive, watched men walk on fiery hot coals in their bare feet, and gone snorkelling in the sparkling clear waters of the Pacific. 'It was wonderful,' she sighed. 'Kevin caught a shark when we went fishing on the reef.'

Kevin did a lot of wonderful things, Lee thought indulgently. Every second sentence was peppered with 'Kevin said . . .' or 'Kevin did . . .' She wondered if she would ever be able to talk so possessively about Tagg. 'I'm glad you had a marvellous time,' she said sincerely. 'What are your plans now?'

Kevin has fixed up the cottage for us on his share of the family property, Brigalow. We're still settling in, but it's fun having a place of my own to decorate and furnish. I never thought of myself as domesticated until now.'

Lee bit her lip. 'I have a favour to ask you.'

'Anything, you know that.'

It seemed she was always asking Karen for help. 'Would you mind taking over the business again sooner than you planned? I know you wanted a bit more time, but it would mean a lot to me if you would.'

'If it's what you want, I'll be glad to.' She wrinkled her nose. 'In a funny way, I've missed the stimulation of the work. But what about you?'

'I'm staying in Walgett until Cheryl is well again. After that, I don't know.'

Karen rested a hand on her arm. 'As long as you don't go back into your shell again.'

'There's no chance. Tagg has given me that much. Steve can't ever hurt me again.'

They were brave words and even as she said them, she wondered if she would come to regret them.

Karen left her outside the hotel, saying she had shopping to do for her new house. Lee watched her go with a feeling of sadness. She looked so happy and contented with her life and with her marriage to Kevin.

Shaking her head at her own folly, Lee went inside. She had no right to begrudge Karen her happiness just because life had been less kind to her.

The hotel receptionist looked puzzled when Lee approached the desk and requested her key. 'Your husband already collected it,' she explained. 'I thought you were expecting him.'

'My husband? Oh ... thank you!'

The receptionist smiled. 'Wish my face still lit up like that when somebody said my husband had arrived.'

Was it so obvious how much she loved Tagg? Her feet barely skimmed the carpeted stairs as she hurried up to her room. He must have regretted his earlier churlishness and decided to surprise her with a visit. Now she could set the record straight and everything would be all right between them.

She was out of breath by the time she pushed open her bedroom door, coming to an abrupt halt as she saw who was stretched out on her bed.

'Steve! What are you doing here?' He lay there as if it was his right. His shoes were off and his tie undone. His jacket swung from a peg behind the door. He smelled of whisky and the expensive cigars he liked to smoke for effect.

'I've come to visit my wife, like I told the lady downstairs,' he drawled.

She pulled the door shut behind her, leaning against it. 'I'm not your wife any more,' she said carefully. 'Even if I hadn't married again, our marriage ended a long time ago. Anything that was left died with Sally.'

'And now there's your fling with the boss of Mundoo.'

'It isn't a fling,' she defended hotly. 'It's . . .' What was it? Since she didn't know herself, she could hardly tell Steve with any conviction.

He arched an eyebrow in the smug fashion she knew only too well. 'So what is it—the love match of the century? Then how come you're here in one miserable hotel room, while he's living in style at the homestead?'

'I'm staying in town to visit a sick friend,' she said angrily, aware of how clichéd it sounded. But it was the truth after all.

'Whatever you say, darling,' he said in a tone meant to placate her.

She was growing tired of this game. 'Would you get off my bed and go away?'

He merely braced his hands behind his head. 'In time, in time. You and I have to talk first.'

'We have nothing left to talk about.'

'Oh, but we do,' he assured her. 'There's a little matter of a police record which I'm sure Mr Laskin would be interested to hear about.'

'No!' Involuntarily, she shrank back against the door. It was like a nightmare, having this happening all over again. She couldn't . . . she wouldn't . . . let him put her through it.

His expression was harder now. 'You never said no to me before.'

'Well, I should have done.' Astonishingly, she felt strength flowing back into her body and mind. It was true! He had no power over her unless she chose to give it to him. 'I should have stood up to you from the first. Cowards can't handle opposition, I'm told.'

His eyes narrowed. 'Are you calling me a coward?'

'What else do you call a man who preys on women just to prove himself the stronger? If it hadn't been for Sally, I would have left a lot sooner but I couldn't leave her with a monster like you, and you knew it. You used my feelings to keep me beside you and make me put up with whatever you felt like handing out. But Sally's gone now and you have no further hold over me. So you can just get out now!'

He regarded her with grudging respect. 'Well, well, so the worm has finally turned.'

'I just want you to go,' she said flatly, feeling exhaustion rather than triumph. 'Haven't you done enough, stealing from Tagg and making him think I'm still involved with you in some way?' Horrified, she clenched her hands together. She hadn't meant to tell him how Tagg had reacted to his visit.

'So maybe he's right.' He held out his arms to her. 'Don't fight it, darling. You don't have anywhere else to go, except to me.'

'Never!' The word came out in a hiss of loathing for him. He had vowed to get her back, or make sure she never knew happiness with another man, and it seemed he was keeping his promise. But no matter how lonely she was, she would never go back to Steve. He was dreaming if he thought so.

Slowly, she inched towards the dresser where a bag of fruit from her breakfast still remained. Beside it was a paring knife she'd bought for the fruit. With a quick gesture, she snatched up the knife and held it out for him to see. 'Now will you leave?'

She saw his resolve weaken fractionally. 'You wouldn't use that?'

'Are you leaving or not?'

Seeing the almost fanatical seriousness with which she held the knife in front of her, he swung his legs off the bed. 'All right, I'm going. No need to get violent.'

This was such a reversal of roles that she almost laughed. For three years she'd been the victim of his behaviour. Now he was worried in case *she* became violent!

She kept her eye on him until he reached the door. As he opened it, she said, 'Next time I see you, I'll let Tagg Laskin turn you in to the police for fraud. I'll even give evidence against you myself. I have nothing to lose any more, Steve.'

For the first time, he looked shaken. Then he shrugged. 'Don't worry, I won't be back. I've had my fun with you. I'm off to greener pastures.'

After the door slammed shut behind him, she sank down on to the bed. Three years of hell, during which he had blackmailed her into doing anything he wanted, and he called it fun? He had used Sally's illness to make her go along with whatever he wanted, including covering up his petty theft. He had even tried to make her shoplift for him, but she had deliberately bungled the attempt so she would be caught. It was the only way she could think of to stop him making her try again.

He had been wrong about the police record, though. When they heard her story, she had been allowed to leave with a caution and Steve had been ordered to stay away from her. She could have called the police about him now, she supposed. But the thought of making a statement and formal charges revolted her. It would mean going over every detail of their past and she couldn't face it again.

It was better this way, having him out of her life for good. She looked at the little paring knife still clutched in her hands. She couldn't have used it, despite her threat. But Steve had believed her, thank goodness. She flung the pathetic weapon on to the dresser.

Steve's visit had done her some good at least, giving her the chance to prove she could stand up to him. In the few weeks she'd known him, Tagg had restored her sense of self-worth. Steve would never take it from her again.

She didn't feel at all like going out again that evening, so she showered and changed into a filmy white négligé and nightdress purchased in a burst of extravagance just before the wedding. It was a far cry from the chaste garment she'd worn that first night at the boundary rider's hut.

Passing the dresser mirror, she caught a glimpse of herself. How ethereal she looked! The garment floated around her like a cloud, touched here and there with tiny embroidered roses. Her hair had grown a little and had begun to curl in the mist from the shower. She flicked the ends up around her face, creating an elfin result.

My God, was this what love could do? Those few days and nights of happiness with Tagg had wrought a wondrous transformation. Her eyes, so recently ringed with violet shadows, shone with a gemlike luminescence that was undoubtedly becoming. And there was a new rosy hue to her cheeks from spending so much time in the open air.

How vain she was getting, she thought as she turned away from the mirror. But it was a welcome change from the self-doubts which had haunted her for the last few years. She had become whole again, and she had Mundoo to thank. No, she had Tagg Laskin to thank, she corrected herself, feeling some of her peace evaporate.

At the same time, she felt a new sense of resolution. Steve was never going to blackmail her with her past again. Tomorrow, she intended to call Tagg and arrange a meeting. Then she would tell him everything. If he despised her for her weakness, she would understand. But at least he would know why she could never be in league with Steve Perry.

There was a tap at her door and she tensed. Surely Steve hadn't come back after all? Nervously, she went to it and spoke through the timber. 'Who is it?'

'It's me, Tagg.'

This time it really was him, and Lee's spirits soared. Her fingers refused to co-operate as she fumbled with the lock but at last she got it open. He stood outside looking achingly handsome in his town gear of polo shirt and drill trousers over polished cowboy boots.

'Hello,' she said, suddenly shy.

'Hello. Aren't you going to invite me in?'

'Yes, please come in.'

Like a polite stranger, Tagg followed her into the room and stood in the middle of the floor, as if uncertain what to do next. 'I went to see Cheryl this afternoon. She said you'd been in this morning,' he said awkwardly.

'She'd appreciate your visit,' Lee said stiffly. Her arms ached to feel his hard body within their circle but she was held back by the uncertainty of her reception. She wasn't even sure why he had come to see her. Maybe—her heart quickened at the thought—maybe he'd come to end it between them.

She felt an urgent need to postpone such news, even if it meant talking about trivialities. 'I ran into Karen this morning,' she said. 'They had a wonderful honeymoon.'

'The one we should have had,' he responded, his voice cracking a little. Then he took a step towards her. 'Oh God, Lee, I don't know what I'm doing here but I had to come.'

She could hardly speak for fear of scaring him away again. 'I'm glad you did.'

'Are you? Did you really miss me?'

'More than anything.' Her body answered in language of its own, swaying towards him so that a half-step brought them into each other's arms.

Tagg kissed her hungrily, his mouth roving over hers as if he needed to rediscover every contour of it. Her heart sang as his arms tightened around her, and she kissed him back with fierce passion.

His hands slid over her shoulders and he slipped open the ribbons tying her négligé, revealing her low-cut nightgown with its border of lace outlining her swelling breasts. His kiss deepened and she gasped as his hands plunged beneath the nightgown, caressing her breasts until her nipples pressed against the filmy fabric.

Under the gown, his hands explored lower and lower until, with an impatient groan, he urged the garment off her shoulders so she stood revealed to him. As the nightgown and négligé fell to her feet, she pressed herself against him. 'Love me, Tagg,' she pleaded, wanting him as she had never wanted anything in her life before.

As he carried her to the bed and laid her carefully on top of it, she marvelled at the desire surging through her. Had she ever been afraid of his lovemaking? It was hard to believe as she welcomed him now.

He looked down at her for a long time, his eyes making love to her, before he kicked off his boots and began to strip off his clothes. As she watched him undressing, her heart swelled with love for him until she could hardly breathe.

At last he stretched out beside her and she kissed him eagerly, moulding her body to his. When they were both aroused beyond endurance, he claimed her at last. But this time, instead of being gently considerate of her fears, he took her with fierce possessiveness which half frightened and half elated her. It was like riding the crest of a powerful tidal wave which swept everything inexorably before it.

Carried on the wave, she cried out in heartfelt joy. There was no fear and no pain, only the unutterable pleasure of his love.

Afterwards, as she lay in the circle of his arms, her head resting on his chest, she said, 'I'm so glad you came back, Tagg.'

'I've been fighting it ever since you telephoned me.'

She looked up at him. 'Why did you decide to come?'

'I told you, I couldn't stay away. For someone who was scared of my touch not so long ago, you're a remarkably sexy lady.'

She pretended annoyance. 'So you really only love me for my body?'

'I wish I knew what I love about you. I was so sure of you until you defended that bastard, Steve Perry. Only after you left, I told myself you hated him. It is the truth, isn't it?'

'Yes, it's true. I had already made up my mind to tell you the truth about Steve and me. It isn't pretty and I'm not proud of it, but you have a right to know.'

He cupped her chin and kissed her forehead lightly. 'You don't have to tell me if you don't want to.'

'But I do want to, otherwise there will always be mistrust between us and Steve could use it against me in future.'

Tagg got out of bed and slipped on his jeans, buckling them, but leaving his chest tantalisingly bare. Then he rummaged in the bag he had brought with him. 'I knew my hunch was right,' he said and pulled out a bottle of wine. 'I bought this on the way up here. Do you have any glasses?'

'Only the tooth mugs on the washstand,' she said. She watched as he opened the bottle and poured the wine, and accepted the cup he handed her.

He settled himself in the only chair, while she wrapped her négligé around herself and piled the pillows behind her. 'Confess away,' he instructed.

She was just wondering where to start when the door burst open and Steve stood there. He must have gone no further than the bar downstairs, judging from the way he clutched at the doorframe for support. He grinned drunkenly when he saw Tagg sitting there, and took in Lee's state of undress. 'This is cosy.'

'What do you want, Perry?' Tagg asked coldly.

He waved a hand uncertainly in the air. 'Nothing, really. I just came for . . . to collect the jacket I left when I was here earlier today.'

Then Lee remembered Steve's jacket which still hung from a peg behind the door. She and Tagg had been so intent on each other that neither of them had noticed it. Now Steve made it sound so incriminating.

Before she could move, Tagg wrenched the jacket off the peg and bundled it into Steve's hands. Then he grasped the other man by the collar and lifted him off his feet, spinning him around so he faced down the corridor. Before Steve knew what was happening, he went sprawling, pushed from behind by Tagg.

'Get the hell out of here and don't show your face again!' Tagg snarled as Steve scrambled to escape.

As Tagg came in again, she heard Steve's whining voice. 'You won't get away with this, Laskin. I swear I'll find a way to get even!' Then the door slammed shut while he was still spitting out threats in a slurred voice.

She blanched when she saw how angry Tagg looked. 'It seems I'm not the first visitor you've had here today,' he said coldly.

'Look, it isn't what you think. He was threatening me again and I ordered him out of my life.'

'It looks like he made himself comfortable while you

were doing it.' Tagg set his drink down carefully and
pulled on his shirt before answering. 'Do I get the same
treatment?'

'No! I love you, Tagg.'

'Then you can get in touch with me as soon as you
decide which husband you really want.'

Before she could overcome her shock to reply, he had
gone. Bleakly, she leaned her forehead against the door.
Damn Steve for coming back just when she and Tagg
were on the verge of an understanding.

And damn Tagg Laskin for believing Steve's lies.

CHAPTER NINE

BY THE time she had typed the last of the day's reports, Lee's arms were aching. It was ages since she'd done any routine office work. Her work at Mundoo had provided endless variety, and working with the computer had spared her the need to type and retype everything.

She sighed, then pulled herself up. She had been lucky to get this job with the local Agricultural Board. Jobs in country towns were scarce and the competition fierce. If they hadn't wanted someone who could start right away, she might not have been so fortunate. The job had been hers for two weeks now.

So why didn't she feel lucky? Distastefully, she looked around the cluttered office. There was only one window which looked on to a lane behind the building. It was a far cry from the vista of trees and rolling paddocks she'd enjoyed at Mundoo.

Damn it! It was time she stopped pining for the place. Tagg had made it clear he didn't want her any more. He hadn't stayed around to hear why Steve had been in her room before he came. Now he believed she was still involved with her ex-husband in some kind of elaborate con game in which Tagg was the victim.

With a savage gesture, Lee tore the paper out of the typewriter and turned the machine off. It was still a couple of minutes to five but her work was finished so she decided to call it a day.

Just as she was locking up the office, the telephone

rang. Reluctantly, she unlatched the door and went to answer it. Her annoyance turned to pleasure when she recognised the voice.

'Cheryl! How are you?'

'If I was any fitter I'd be dangerous,' came the reply. 'But since they put me in this outpatients' cottage, I'm going out of my mind with boredom.'

'Won't they let you go home to Mundoo?'

She could imagine Cheryl's candyfloss hair swinging as she shook her head. 'No way. I'm supposed to stay here till the baby's born. It isn't so bad at weekends when Ray and Craigie come to stay, but the weekdays drag on for ever.'

Pangs of guilt assailed Lee. She had been a regular visitor while Cheryl was in hospital, but her visits became fewer after Cheryl was discharged. 'Would you like me to come over and see you?' she asked.

'What about this evening? I'll cook us some dinner.'

'Will that be all right?'

Cheryl laughed. 'Of course. I have the cottage to myself and it's equipped as a home from home.'

'In that case, I'll see you at six.'

Uncertain of her future, Lee was still living at the hotel, although she was growing tired of her one-room existence. Every morning she promised herself that today she would look for a house or a flat, but found plenty of excuses to put it off.'

As she dressed for her evening with Cheryl, she knew why she wasn't eager to find a new home. She didn't want to remain in the area if she couldn't be with Tagg. Knowing he was so near, yet being unable to see him or share his life, was pure agony. He had made no attempt to contact her after Steve's fateful reappearance.

Involuntarily, her gaze strayed to the double bed where Tagg had last made love to her. Her body ached at the memory of his touch and the fiery possessiveness with which he had claimed her. It was inconceivable that she would never know such ecstasy again.

The outpatients' cottage was set in its own garden a short distance from the main hospital. Apart from a side gate which led into the hospital grounds, it could have been a private one.

'As I said, home from home,' Cheryl repeated when she opened the front door.

The two women hugged each other. 'I'm sorry about not visiting,' Lee said. 'I'm working in town now.'

'I know, at the Agricultural Board.'

'I'd forgotten that I'm talking to Reuters,' Lee laughed and followed Cheryl into the cottage.

The interior was compact, with two bedrooms looking out on to the gardens, and a combined living and dining-room with an open-plan kitchen beyond it. The décor was impersonal but cosy, with chintz curtaining and pretty floral cretonne covers on the armchairs. Cheryl had set out tea things and biscuits on a tray in the living-room.

When they were seated, Cheryl said, 'Do you know, you're the first visitor I've had from Mundoo all week!'

'But not your only visitor, surely?' Lee asked, surprised.

'Oh no, I've had most of Walgett through that front door, but it isn't the same, somehow.' Her voice held a wistful quality.

'Then I'm here under false pretences, because I haven't been to Mundoo for two weeks,' Lee admitted.,

Cheryl busied herself pouring their tea. Without

looking up, she said, 'I know. I wanted to talk to you about that.'

'There's nothing you can do,' Lee said quickly. 'Tagg and I had a difference of opinion and we . . . we decided we're not really suited to marriage, that's all.'

'Then you're both crazy,' Cheryl said flatly. 'I never saw two people more in love.'

One person, Lee thought bleakly. Tagg couldn't love her, or he wouldn't condemn her without even giving her a chance to explain. She sipped her tea thoughtfully. 'How's the baby?' she asked at last.

Cheryl patted her rounded stomach, clearly evident under her floral maternity dress. 'It has to be a boy because he spends so much time at football practice. He kicks a lot,' she explained when Lee looked puzzled. 'But I don't mind. When I think what could have happened . . .'

'Don't think about it,' Lee urged. 'You're in good hands now and nothing's going to go wrong.'

They talked for a while about Lee's new job. Cheryl knew her boss well and was interested in Lee's experience of working for him. Since Cheryl hadn't yet been able to visit Karen's new home, she was also anxious to hear all about it. Lee had been to visit the newly-weds the previous weekend.

When Lee described Karen's decorating efforts, Cheryl sighed enviously. 'I feel so out of touch being cooped up here. I'm only supposed to go out for "gentle exercise",' she said quoting the doctor acidly.

'You still manage to keep well informed,' Lee laughed. 'You knew about my new job, for instance.'

'Well, I have to do *something* to keep my mind active,' Cheryl said plaintively.

She had been keeping her hands active by preparing an excellent meal, Lee discovered. The cottage larder was apparently well stocked by a local grocer and deliveries were charged to the patient's bill. It was an ideal way of looking after people who were too well to be in hospital but still needed on-going medical care.

'Parents of sick children often stay here, rather than make the long trip back and forth from their properties,' Cheryl explained. 'I'm the only tenant at the moment.'

They started their meal with slices of chilled melon, followed by grilled steaks with pepper sauce and a cherry brandy cake which Ray had brought as a present for his wife. 'Isn't Ray marvellous?' Cheryl enthused. 'He brings me little things every time he comes, when I'm happy enough just to see him.'

A pang shot through Lee. Karen and Kevin . . . Cheryl and Ray . . . it seemed as if the whole world came in pairs and she was the only odd one out.

Cheryl reached for her hand. 'I know what you're thinking. But a good marriage takes work, on both sides.'

'I'm willing. But Tagg isn't.'

'Are you sure about that?'

Remembering Tagg's implacable expression when he left the hotel, Lee nodded. 'I don't think he wants to see me again.'

Cheryl poured her a glass of wine, while sipping soda herself. 'Would it help to tell me about it?'

Her tone was so compassionate that the dam of emotion Lee had been holding back burst forth in a torrent of words. She found herself telling Cheryl all about Sally's losing battle for survival; how she had given up work to be with her. 'We had no money, so I couldn't take her away,' she said. 'I had to go along with Steve because he might have hurt Sally.'

'You poor kid,' Cheryl said sympathetically. 'But there's more, isn't there?'

'Yes,' she admitted in a low voice. 'Soon after we were married I saw another side to him. Little things used to irritate him out of all proportion, and he used to get these—these black moods. Especially after Sally was born. After she became so ill I never used to see even a hint of the old Steve. I could hardly remember why I'd fallen in love with him. And sometimes it wasn't just words he abused me with ... he ... he ...'

'He got violent?' Cheryl guessed. 'Oh, Lee, if only you knew how common it is in marriages. I've known women who put up with violent husbands for years, without even a child as a reason for staying.'

Having started, Lee felt compelled to unburden herself completely. 'It was worse than that,' she said in a voice barely above a whisper. 'One day, when he had spent our mortgage money on gambling, he ... he ordered me to steal from a department store for him. He hid Sally's medicine and said I wouldn't get it back till I co-operated.'

'And you knew what he was capable of, so you did what he said.'

Shame made Lee's cheeks burn. 'I nearly did, but I couldn't go through with it. The only thing I could think of was to let myself get caught so Steve couldn't force me to try again. Luckily, the police were very kind. They spoke to Steve for me. He was furious but he couldn't do much with them watching him. Then after Sally died ... we seemed to get a little closer, but it didn't last. He soon reverted to type.'

Cheryl nodded in understanding. 'That's when you decided to get out?'

'Not soon enough, I see that now. But Steve sapped my self-confidence to such a degree, I started to doubt whether I could make it on my own. It took friends like Karen Vaughan and my doctor, Marie Mather, to help me see that Steve was the weak one, not me.'

Cheryl walked around the table and grasped Lee's shoulders, holding her tightly. 'You poor kid. Did you tell Tagg any of this?'

'Only the part about Sally. I was too afraid of losing his respect if he found out how weak I'd been.'

'So he has no idea what really happened between you and Steve Perry?' Lee nodded. 'No wonder he thinks the worst.' She returned to her seat. 'You have to tell him the truth. You do want him back, don't you?'

'Of course, but I'm afraid once he knows what sort of person I am, he'll despise me even more.'

'What sort of person you *were*,' Cheryl emphasised. 'In any case, you're wrong. You were just too young to know what your options were. As soon as you realised, you got out, so you can't be as weak as you think. My guess is that you want to tell Tagg the truth. Even if he does take it badly, you won't be worse off than you are now. So what are you waiting for?'

Feeling as if a great burden had been lifted off her shoulders, Lee smiled at Cheryl. 'You're right. I do want our marriage to work. Tomorrow is my day off, so I'll go out to Mundoo and see him.'

'That's the spirit!' Cheryl held out a bunch of keys on a chain. 'You can even borrow my car, since I'm not going anywhere.'

* * *

Next day, the sun was shining in sympathy with Lee's mood as she set off in Cheryl's Holden station waggon. Luckily it was an automatic gear-change model, so she was soon accustomed to driving it and only had to worry about recognising the turn-off which led to the homestead.

Her stomach was churning by the time she pulled up outside the imposing old building with its ancient cedar trees standing like sentinels at the front. How dear and familiar it looked now! Her gaze went to the small building at the end of the covered walkway. Tagg might be in his office at this moment.

The thought provoked a feeling of panic. Why hadn't she telephoned ahead to let Tagg know she was coming? She had avoided calling in case he refused to see her—and he *had* to see her.

'Hello, Mrs Laskin. Good to see you back.'

Under the broad-brimmed bushman's hat, she recognised Bill Drury, the stockman who had interrupted their honeymoon with the news of Cheryl's illness. 'Hi, Bill,' she said.

'How is Mrs di Falco?' he asked before she could enquire about Tagg.

'She's doing well,' she said a little impatiently. 'They're keeping her in Walgett for observation until the baby is born. Didn't Ray tell you?'

Bill pushed the hat to the back of his head. 'Haven't seen him for a couple of days. He and the boss went out to the experimental paddock, checking on their new strain of grass. They've been gone for a couple of days.'

She leaned against the car, disappointment overwhelming her. 'When will they be back?'

'They didn't say. Seems a long time to be checking

one paddock but that's what they said they were doing.'

Damn Tagg and his quest for the perfect stock feed to drought-proof his precious property, she thought angrily. Then she realised she was being foolish. Tagg didn't know she was coming, so she couldn't blame him for being busy when she arrived.

A sudden impulse revived her spirits. 'Could you direct me to the experimental paddock?' she asked.

Bill looked doubtful. 'The track's a bit rough out that way. I doubt whether you could drive it in that car.'

She was not to be dissuaded now. 'In that case, I'll ride over,' she said. 'Can you organise a horse for me? I'll go and change.'

Although obviously reluctant, Bill deferred to her position as mistress of the station, however nebulous her role might be. As she went into the house, he walked off towards the home paddock. Looking back, she saw him aproach a grey gelding she'd ridden with Tagg when she was here before.

Half an hour later, she emerged dressed in moleskins and a long-sleeved cotton shirt. A straw sun-hat dangled around her neck. Luckily she had left most of her clothes here in the rush to get Cheryl to hospital. Living in town, she hadn't needed most of them and had been unable to summon the courage to ask Tagg to send them to her. Now she was glad.

Bill was waiting outside, holding her horse which was saddled and ready. 'Would you like me to come with you?' he asked.

Lee dared not add to Tagg's annoyance with her by taking one of his key men away from his duties. 'No, thank you.' she said. 'Just tell me which way to go and I'll be fine.' She listened attentively as he gave her the directions. Since most of the tracks were faint or non-existent, she wondered if she was doing the right thing, but she was committed now. 'I'll find them,' she said with more assurance than she felt.

The ride was surprisingly pleasant once she relaxed and began to work with her horse. The wavering cattle track meandered between stands of tall eucalypts. The black shadows beneath them contrasted with the bleached brightness of the paddocks. In the chasms, mobs of sheep had made their camp for the day. They wouldn't come out to graze until the cool of the evening.

Gradually, the track wound up the side of a ridge which divided Mundoo from north to south. It was low in contrast with the Warrumbungle ranges to the south, but it was the highest point on the property and when she crested it, Mundoo lay like a patchwork quilt beneath her.

The homestead itself was invisible, cloaked by a stand of trees which stood between her and the house. She might have been the only human being on earth.

After an hour's riding, she dismounted and let her horse graze on grass along a wire fence, dropping the reins over its head to stop it straying. Then she leaned against the taut strands and drank in the fragrance of the wildflowers, hearing the drone of a thousand insects in her ears. The flowers were already wilting, having blossomed in the rains. Tagg had told her the seeds could lie dormant in the soil for as long as ten years, waiting for good rain to bring them to life. Then they lived and died in an all-too brief but glorious span.

Sighing, she mounted up again and looked around, trying to remember Bill's exact instructions.

There was supposed to be a gate in this fence, she

remembered, annoyed with herself because she couldn't
see it. She decided to follow the fence until she came to
the break. Beyond it she had to cross another paddock
which ended in a gravel creek bed. Tagg's camp was
supposed to be on the other side.

Her sense of loneliness increased sharply. A wedge-
tailed eagle wheeled overhead and a goanna paused
stonily up a tree, its flickering tongue the only sign that
it was alive. She gave it a grateful glance, thankful for
any sign of life, and rode onwards.

The sun was scorching and she was glad of the straw
hat which protected her head. Would she never find the
break in the fence?

She located it at last, although much further on than
Bill had indicated. Urging the horse to a faster pace, she
crossed the paddock, looking for the dry creek bed.

Abruptly, she emerged from a thick stand of eucalypts
into what was unmistakably a camp. There were a
couple of canvas tents set up and a makeshift corral
which contained a number of bleating merinos. Tagg
must be working with the sheep as well as tending to his
experiments, she thought.

At the camp, she unsaddled the horse and rubbed the
saddle grime from his back, then turned him into the
makeshift corral, where he rolled in the grass with great
ecstasy.

Between the tents, several sheets of cast iron were
arranged in a square and contained the remnants of a fire
and several blackened cooking pots and a billy. She
touched the ashes. They were cold. Tagg and Ray had
been gone for some time.

They wouldn't normally return to camp for lunch,
she recalled. Most of the men ate sandwiches from their

saddle-bags, and a thermos of coffee or a billy of tea on the hob. They needed to be all-rounders, able to cook for themselves, tend their animals, use an axe or chainsaw to mend fences, repair vehicles, and if needed, shoe their horses as well, so they had no need of pampering.

Parked in the shade of a coolibah was an ex-army truck she hadn't noticed when she rode in. It contained supplies, grain sacks and food boxes—surely more than two men needed on a short trip. She didn't recognise the truck but perhaps it belonged to another of Tagg's men. Motorbike tracks led away from the truck across a nearby dry creek.

Her tour of inspection completed, she sat down in the shade and opened the packet of sandwiches Bill had urged on her before he saw her off. She washed them down with water from her canteen, making a face when she discovered it was lukewarm. Still, water was precious out here so she carefully screwed the lid back on and replaced it in her saddle-bag.

The sun was still high so she didn't expect Tagg and Ray to return for several hours. Debating whether to lie down in the shade of the tree, she decided to use one of the tents. At least she would be safe from snakes and spiders on a stretcher.

One tent was apparently used for supplies. In the other was a pair of wooden stretchers with sleeping bags unrolled on top of them. Which one was Tagg's? she wondered, then chided herself for being sentimental. She felt like Goldilocks in the three bears' cottage. Which bed would be just right?

In the end, she dropped on to the nearest one and tossed her hat on to the floor. Although it was hot and airless in the tent, the canvas walls gave her an illusion of security and she was soon asleep.

The trip from town and the ride had tired her and she slept deeply, her dreams disturbed. Steve and Tagg were fighting a duel over her. It was a crazy dream because Tagg was dressed in modern-day cowboy gear and sat tall on a raw-boned stockman's horse. Steve was on foot, so the match was unequal, especially since Tagg wielded a stockman's whip and Steve fought back with a double-barrelled shotgun used as a club.

Wanting to escape from the dream, she stirred restlessly in the cot. Distantly, she heard Steve's voice and that of another man. Why wouldn't the dream go away?

Then she awoke properly and rubbed her eyes. It was dark and the tent was inky black with only a shaft of moonlight spilling through the front flap and across the floor. She must have been asleep for hours.

The sound of voices outside the tent disturbed her and she rolled over on to her back to listen. Tagg and Ray must have returned while she slept.

Then the tent flap parted, outlining a tall man in silhouette. Her heart leapt. Tagg was back! In the same instant she realised just how wrong she was. The man in the tent wasn't Tagg at all. She would know that hated profile anywhere. It was Steve Perry. What on earth was he doing in a camp, out here on Tagg's land?

She froze, her mind whirling. If she lay still he might go to sleep on the other bunk, then she could creep out undiscovered.

As she watched, he dropped something on to the other bed, a saddle-bag she guessed from the dull thud as it landed. In the darkness it was hard to make out more than his dim outline but she saw him begin to undress.

His shirt, jeans and boots landed in a heap on the floor and as he bent to move them aside, the moonlight slanted off his body, although his features remained in darkness.

Her breathing quickened as she watched him move about the tent. If only he didn't light the hurricane lamp she had noticed swinging from the tent pole when she arrived, he wouldn't ever know she had been here.

But luck was against her. With a sinking heart she watched him lift the lamp down and fiddle with it. She gathered herself to make a run for it.

Before she could move, the flame sputtered and caught, throwing the interior of the tent into golden relief. Steve moved like lightning, pinning her to the cot with a grip of steel.

'You think I didn't know you were here?' he said nastily. 'What I want to know is why.'

'I thought this was Tagg's camp,' she said, fighting against his grip.

'Did you now?' he drawled. 'Well, now you're here, you're going to stay here.' He grasped her with an iron grip that bit into her flesh.

'No!' She strained against his hold and it loosened enough for her to free one hand. Flailing at his face, she left a trail of nail marks down his cheek. As soon as he clutched at the wound, she leapt off the bed.

But he was quicker. Before she reached the tent flap, he brought her to the ground in a flying tackle which knocked all the breath out of her. 'You bitch, I'll teach you to scratch me!' Dragging her back to the cot, he threw her on to it.

As she struggled to rise, he clamped her wrists either side of her head so she couldn't move. 'You're not going anywhere,' he vowed. 'If Laskin is around here somewhere, we can't have you telling him what you've seen.'

'I haven't seen anything,' she lied, trying to buy time. 'I don't even know what you're doing here.'

'But you've seen the camp and the sheep in that little pen by the creek,' he said. 'What do you think me and my mate are doing with them?'

Suddenly she understood. All the supplies, the cattle truck and the motorbike added up to one thing. 'You're stealing Tagg's sheep!'

'As if you hadn't already guessed,' he said nastily. 'Of course we're bloody stealing them! Without his prize breeding stock, his stock won't be quite so valuable, will it? Especially if we put a torch to his precious Mundoo on our way out.'

'You've thought of everything, haven't you?' she said grimly, her brain registering only one thing. They were going to burn out Mundoo and she had to get to Tagg in time to prevent it.

'Too right we have. Those beasts in the pen represent the pick of Laskin's stock. My mate outside is very knowledgeable about sheep, you see. He used to work on this property until he and the boss had a ... a misunderstanding. So he has a vested interest in getting his own back, like me.'

'And what about me?' she asked, already afraid of the answer.

'You're a bonus I didn't expect. I was trying to think of a way of fixing you after you let the boyfriend throw me out of your room. Now you can be our passport out of here.'

Fear stabbed through her. Spread-eagled on the cot,

Lee felt terribly vulnerable and a wave of revulsion washed over her. 'You're talking about kidnapping,' she reminded him, keeping her voice level with an effort.

He laughed harshly. 'Now how would you prove it?' he asked. 'Given that we were married, and I've been seen in your room at the hotel? Laskin already thinks you're still on with me.'

Ignoring her struggles, he slipped the belt of his jeans off, grasped her wrists and wound the belt around them, then jerked her bound hands over her head and buckled them to the frame of the cot. 'That should take care of you for now. If you have any ideas about screaming for help, forget them, unless you'd like me to gag you as well.'

The idea terrified her and she kept silent. He watched her for a moment then went out of the tent, dropping the flap behind him. She heard him talking to the other man—the mate he had mentioned. There was a short argument and she wondered if she was the cause. But Steve didn't come back, and she heard the clink of bottles as they settled around the campfire to eat and drink.

Her arms ached from being bound above her head and she tested the bond. The bed creaked and she froze, but no one came. There was the clink of more bottles, and harsh laughter. Maybe Steve would get drunk and forget about her for long enough to let her escape.

More cautiously this time, she worked at the belt holding her hands. It was almost loose enough to slide her hands through. With a little more effort . . .

The skin of her wrists was chafed and sore by the time she loosened the belt enough to get both hands free, and she massaged them as pins and needles invaded her arms.

When she was sure the men hadn't heard her struggles she crept to the tent entrance. In the flickering glow of the firelight, she could see them crouched on logs, drinking from bottles. They had lost interest in her for the time being.

Since the tent opened directly on to the clearing where they sat, she couldn't go out that way. So she went to the back of the tent and worked the back wall up far enough to allow her to wriggle underneath.

There was no question of releasing her horse which was in the paddock with the stolen sheep. She would have to get away on foot and trust that Steve was right and Tagg was somewhere close by.

The bush, which had seemed so friendly when she rode in, now seemed menacing with its myriad rustling sounds. All around her, nocturnal animals hurried through the undergrowth. An owl glided silently overhead then darted to the ground in front of her and streaked away, a squirming meal in its beak.

She had only gone a few hundred yards when she heard a cry of dismay from Steve's camp. He must have gone to the tent to check up on her, and found her missing.

Crashing sounds behind her warned her that Steve and his mate were searching the area for her. They couldn't call out for fear of alerting Tagg, but neither could she without attracting Steve's attention. So she froze, making herself invisible against the insect-scarred trunk of a red gum.

A man passed within feet of her without seeing her, although she was afraid he would hear her laboured breathing and the terrified thump-thump of her aching heart. But he went away and she heard the two men arguing, each blaming the other for her escape.

When she was sure they had given up the search, she slipped off through the bush, wanting to put as much distance between herself and Steve as possible.

By the time she felt safe enough to stop for rest, the first hint of dawn was streaking the sky. Exhausted and shivering, she watched as the soft light slowly flooded the purple land and spilled across the bleached pastures. As soon as the light touched the eerie outlines of the eucalypts, the birds burst into song.

Suddenly the air was alive with the laughing cries of kookaburras, the screech and twitter of parrots and the car-car of crows. Overhead, a flock of wild ducks V-planed towards their favourite watering hole.

She greeted the light with relief but some trepidation. She wasn't sure just how far she had come during the night. If it wasn't as far as she imagined, daylight would make her an easy target. She had to find Tagg's camp before Steve found her.

CHAPTER TEN

SHE had been walking for what seemed like ages, but the thin strands of wire fencing bordering the paddock seemed to be no closer. Every time something moved in the underbrush, she started with fear. Was it Steve or his friend, come to drag her back with them? But it was usually only a grey-faced wallaby, peeping at her, unafraid, from behind the trees, or a spiny anteater, scrabbling away, more frightened of her than she was of him.

If only she had waited at the homestead for Tagg to return, she wouldn't be in this mess now. But she had been so anxious to set things right between them. She had never dreamed that Steve would try something like this.

Somehow, the thought of him as a sheep stealer didn't surprise her. Nothing he did could do that any more. He had long ago destroyed any illusions she harboured about him. To other people, he was a healthy, joking type who was always good for a laugh. Inwardly, he was insecure and needed constant reassurance. If he didn't get it, or it wasn't enough to satisfy him, he turned violent and took his own fears out on her in aggressive behaviour.

He was the younger of two brothers. His older brother, Andrew, was their parents' darling: brighter, stronger and better-looking, excelling at everything and leaving Steve to trail in his shadow. This frustration, she was sure, accounted for his present behaviour.

Steve had tried to escape, leaving his parents' property in the country to start anew as a machinery salesman in the city, where Lee met him. But he couldn't escape himself and when city life proved to be no better or worse than country life, he had taken his frustration out on her or by gambling recklessly and keeping them constantly in debt. He had had to wear down her self-confidence because his own was so low—and yet, when he had succeeded in humiliating her, he had come to despise her. It was a vicious circle; he had accused her time and again of failing as a wife, until she had come to believe him. Everything she did had seemed to make him angry. Sally's arrival hadn't changed him, only providing him with another hold over Lee.

She pushed a hand through her hair which was sticky with perspiration. What was the good of going over it all now? Steve was driven by demons she couldn't begin to understand. She had done the only thing she could, which was to get out and try to start her life anew.

She laughed hollowly. She hadn't been very successful there, either. Her marriage to Tagg Laskin, agreed to as a means of escape from Steve's persecution, had turned into something much more serious. He was the man Steve could never be—competent, self-assured enough to be tender and compassionate. If only she had trusted him enough to tell him about her past, Steve wouldn't have been able to come between them.

Her thoughts chased themselves in circles like bees around a hive, until she cried aloud with annoyance. Her throat was parched and every breath emphasised her thirst, drawing hot, dry air into her throat and lungs. Her legs ached from all the walking, but she daren't stop to rest until she was sure she was safe.

Reaching the wire strands at last, she pushed her weary body over them, almost crying when her shirt caught in a twist of wire. Wrenching it free, she tore it and left the streamer of fabric trapped in the wire. No longer caring, she pushed onwards, stumbling over rabbit holes and rain-washed runnels.

Cresting a rise, she came upon a grove of gum trees, standing bare-leaved, like sentinels. There was something familiar about them, if only she could recall what it was. Then she remembered.

Running and stumbling towards them, she clasped her arms around a weird S-shaped eucalypt. Her cheek was on a level with some initials carved deep into the bark, their edges softened and blurred by time, but still clearly legible. 'TL loves AH'.

She had found Tagg's boyhood hiding place.

Forgetting how jealous she had been when she first saw Tagg with the other woman, she blessed Adora Hamilton for coming here with him when they were children.

The boundary rider's hut couldn't be far away from here, and near it, the road between Mundoo and Robina.

Not much further on, she located the creek where Tagg had taken her swimming, although the cabin was nowhere in sight. Disorientated by thirst and exhaustion, she wasn't sure in which direction it lay from here.

All the same, the sight of the sparkling water, garlanded by wild birds enjoying their morning drink, was enough to reduce her to tears of gratitude. Surely Tagg would find her here.

As she approached, the birds rose in great flurries of wings and she was treated to a splendid display of white

and pink galahs, and the rainbow hues of the lorrikeets.
High above her, in the branches of a red gum, a
kookaburra burst into raucous laughter.

She smiled up at him. 'Thanks, I know how you feel!'

Cupping her hands, she drank the gritty water which
tasted like the finest champagne as it ran down her
parched throat. Her thirst finally slaked, she sat down on
the bank, bracing her back against a tree. Was it really
only a few weeks since she and Tagg had made love here
on the riverbank?

She had a sudden vivid recollection of how splendid
he had looked, like a god rising out of the river, the
droplets cascading off his brown, sculptured body. A
feverish sensation seared her. He had taught her that
lovemaking should bring pleasure, not pain, and now
she craved that pleasure like an addict.

Was it only his lovemaking she missed? No, she had to
confess that he had brought much more into her life
than physical pleasure. Although she yearned to feel his
arms around her, and his voice whispering that he loved
her, there was so much they could share. They both
loved the Australian bush and the farming life; they
were both romantics—Tagg with his love of tradition;
she with her penchant for orange blossom perfume.
They could have such a good life together, if only they
could both learn to trust again.

As the sun climbed higher in the sky, the air
temperature crept upwards until she was bathed in a
film of perspiration. Through the lacy covering of
leaves, the sun scorched the top of her head. Her sunhat
was on the floor of Steve's tent.

Around her the paddocks began to shimmer and

dance, and a lake appeared in the distance. She resisted
the urge to walk towards it, knowing there would be
nothing but grey dust when she got there. The creek was
real, and she would be foolish to leave its sanctuary. She
thought she knew which way the cabin lay, but she was
afraid to take the risk of getting lost again. Far better to
stay where she was.

A wave of dizziness washed over her and she forced
her head down. Exhaustion, lack of food—she'd eaten
nothing since the sandwiches yesterday—were making
her feel faint. The bush took on an air of unreality.

In her dazed state of mind, she imagined that Tagg
had found her and was standing looking down at her.
'My God, Lee—are you all right?'

She mumbled something, having difficulty forming
the words, and he dropped to his knees beside her. He
had wrung out a handkerchief in cool water and bathed
her forehead with it. 'Feels good,' she murmured. It was
only a dream, but she could almost feel the droplets
trickling down her face and when she opened her
mouth, her questing tongue found some of the water
and licked it.

'I love you,' she said.

'I love you too, you crazy, adorable woman.'

'Not crazy.'

'Well, adorable, anyway.'

'This is my dream, you can't insult me,' she said
stubbornly.

The dream image smiled and his skin crinkled into
furrows each side of that oh-so-kissable mouth. She felt
her insides constrict. 'Where are you, Tagg?' she asked,
shutting her eyes.

'I'm right here, my darling, right here.'

This was too silly for words. She knew she was on the verge of sunstroke which could make one delirious, but dream images weren't supposed to talk back to you. She decided to ignore it, and try to sleep.

The sensation of being carried woke her and she looked up to find herself cradled in Tagg's arms, held tight against the hardness of his chest. If this was a dream, she didn't want it to end.

Still dazed, she let herself be lowered on to a wide, blissfully comfortable bed, feeling the coolness of sheets beneath her. Then gentle hands eased her jeans off and cool air brushed her legs, freed of the heavy material. When the hands went to her shirt buttons, she felt as though she should protest, but it was only a dream, so what did it matter?

She allowed her shirt to be taken off, then her bra and finally, her lace briefs were eased down around her hips and removed altogether. She lay naked and uncaring, floating in her dream-state.

She had no doubt that she was still under the red gum, beside the creek. This was just a wonderful fantasy her mind had conjured up because it was what she wanted more than anything else—Tagg beside her, ministering to her with his tender, teasing touch.

A shiver ran down her spine as a damp cloth touched her legs, the sensation amazingly vivid. Then she became aware of the steady pressure of the cloth as it moved up and down her limbs, bathing every inch of her with coolness. Waves of pleasure assailed her as the cloth was drawn gently over her stomach and thighs, the touch tantalising by its very lightness. Then her breasts were bathed and she felt her nipples spring to alertness as the slightly rough cloth teased at them.

As her skin temperature fell, the dreamlike sensation started to lift and she opened her eyes. She wasn't dreaming! She was lying on the bed in the boundary rider's hut, and Tagg was really here.

'Hello, sleepy-eyes,' he said, noticing that she was stirring.

'Am I still dreaming?' she asked uncertainly.

He carried the cloth back and reached for her hand, placing it against the bony side of his hip. 'Feel me, I'm real enough. You nearly had sunstroke, but I think I found you in time.'

'I feel wonderful,' she said languorously. 'It's ages since anyone gave me a sponge bath.'

'I hope it was someone with a medical degree, otherwise I may have to find him and demand satisfaction,' he growled.

'It was a her,' she smiled, 'and I was fourteen and in hospital having my appendix out.'

He traced a line along her stomach, sending eddies of desire whirling through her. 'So that explains the trace of a scar. I was wondering about it.'

He set to work with the cloth again, this time caressing her so intimately that she knew he was no longer trying to bring her temperature down. In fact, it was having the opposite effect. Her pulses raced and her heart felt as though it was going to beat right out of her chest. If he didn't make love to her soon, she would explode.

As he leant over her she clasped her arms around his neck, drawing him down so she could kiss the mouth which had been teasing her so in her dream. But this time, they were both wide awake and his response was every bit as satisfying, yet demanding as she had fantasised.

Her quivering fingers twined through his hair as his lips worked at her mouth, then he left a trail of kisses along her jawline and down to the sensitive hollow of her throat. Burying his face between her neck and shoulder, he let his free hand rove over the rest of her, until she was one quivering, mindless mass of desire.

She was on fire with love for him, wanting only the fulfilment of his possession. Later, they would talk, but now they had something much more primal to share.

This time, when he made love to her, there was no holding back. Instinctively she knew just how to move subtly, to give him as much pleasure as he was giving her. His heaving breath contained only her name, repeated over and over. 'Alita, Alita, Alita.'

Could any man say her name with such sweetness and warmth as Tagg Laskin could?

She was a volcano, primed to explode in a boiling, blinding turmoil. Suddenly, all remaining doubts and fears were swept away in a molten wave of sensation which obliterated everything but the two of them. Together, they remade the world.

'Is this the same Alita who used to tremble when I touched her?' Tagg asked in wonder, when they lay side by side in the dreamy aftermath.

'You said yourself, I'm a fast learner.'

'Only with me?'

A stab of dismay went through her. She had foolishly believed the last few minutes had meant as much to him as they did to her. 'You know the answer to that,' she said tautly.

'Do I, Alita?' He sat up and swung his legs over the

side of the bed, hunching over to rest his forearms on his knees. 'I wish to God I did.'

How could he say such a cruel thing after carrying her to such dizzying heights of pleasure? Was sex all they shared, after all? 'You must believe I love you,' she said dully.

He didn't look at her. 'I don't know what to believe any more. After finding your hat and saddle-bag at the rustlers' camp . . .'

'You found them?' she said, sitting up.

'Yes. I don't know of any easy way to tell you but your ex-husband is on his way to gaol at this very minute.'

Her response was automatic. 'Thank God!'

This time, he regarded her with an odd mixture of fear and uncertainty. 'Do you really mean that? You're pleased about it?'

'Of course. When I stumbled on them trying to steal your stud ewes . . .'

He broke in impatiently. 'Wait a minute. You stumbled on them—does that mean you weren't trying to find Steve Perry, after all?'

'Of course not. I never wanted to see him again. It was you I was looking for.'

'Me? What for?'

She twisted the sheet between nervous fingers. 'I haven't been really honest with you, Tagg. I thought it was time you knew all about me so we could start again—if you wanted to, that is. It took so much courage to come out to Mundoo that when they told me you were out on the property, I knew if I didn't go after you straight away, I'd lose my nerve altogether.'

'Am I so much of an ogre?'

She smiled. 'Far from it. But I *am* a coward. I tried to

follow Bill Drury's directions—I still don't know where
I went wrong. But I stumbled into the rustlers' camp
instead of yours.'

Tagg's face looked grey. 'I thought you were looking
for Perry because you couldn't live without him. Until I
found out what he'd done to you ...'

She stared at him, wide-eyed. 'You know about that?'

'Yes.' He massaged the knuckles of his right hand. 'It
took a bit of persuading but I finally got it out of him.'

'You fought him?'

He grinned ruefully. 'It was a very one-sided fight,
but I knew I'd never get the chance to be alone with him
again, and I had to know what went on between you to
make you so frightened of commitment.'

'And now you know. I don't blame you for despising
me ...' she said quickly.

He stared at her. 'I don't despise you. Whatever gives
you that idea?'

'You must think me terribly weak and spineless,
married to a man like that for three years.'

He took her by the upper arms, turning her to face
him. 'You had your baby to think of. I wouldn't expect
you to leave a child with a bastard like Perry. And I know
as well as anyone that we don't always have a choice in
how we live our lives. You see, when the courts gave my
mother custody, I didn't want to leave Australia,
although I later came to love Texas, but I know that
often, we have to live in the grip of forces stronger than
ourselves. I believe it was like that for you.'

She nodded, marvelling at his understanding. 'That's
how I felt. He gambled so much that I never had enough
money to take Sally away and give her the care she
needed. Steve threatened that if I left he would find us

and make sure no man would ever want us. I think he meant to ... scar me in some way.'

'He very nearly did, but not in the way you mean,' Tagg said grimly. 'I should have killed the bastard when I had the chance.'

'No, Tagg, don't even think it. You can't cure violence with violence. I know you can take care of yourself, you don't have to prove anything to me.'

'I suppose not. But when I think of Perry ill-treating you ...'

'It's all right,' she interposed softly, closing her hand around his clenched fist. 'If it hadn't been for Sally, I would have left him a lot sooner.' She looked away. 'You know my parents were against our getting married in the first place. I could have gone to them, I know, but they couldn't have coped with a child as ill as Sally was. And I had nowhere else to go.'

'Is that where Karen came in?' he asked. 'I noticed how close you two are.'

'She's closer to me than either of my sisters,' Lee explained. 'After Sally died, she was a great comfort. When I made up my mind to leave, she sent me money and gave me a friend's address so I could get away from Steve long enough to start divorce proceedings.'

'And then she quietly eloped so you and I would be thrown together,' he said. 'Karen has a lot to answer for.'

'She denies that was the reason why she ran off, but I think she was trying to matchmake,' Lee said almost shyly.

'Are you sorry?'

Emphatically, she shook her head. 'No, are you?'

'No. I was strongly attracted to you that first time we

met at Karen's party, but you were such a mixture of nun and coquette, I didn't know what to make of you. I was furious when it looked like you were using me to make another man jealous, but I couldn't get you out of my mind. When you turned up at Walgett, I thought I'd been given a second chance.'

'We both had,' she said softly. 'Is that why you were so keen to marry me?'

'You guessed my secret,' he laughed. 'I wanted you to think I was a knight in shining armour, rescuing you from your wicked ex-husband, but I really wanted to marry you for my own selfish reasons.'

Her gaze softened. 'I'm glad. I'd hate to think you married me because you felt sorry for me.'

'No, never that.'

She sat up and bent her knees, hugging her arms around them. 'You still haven't explained how you found me.'

'You left a trail.' He fished in his pocket and pulled out a scrap of cloth. 'I found this clinging to the fence, so I knew which way you'd headed.'

It was almost as if she'd wanted to leave a trail for him, she reflected dreamily. 'What happened to Steve and the other man?' she asked curiously.

'Ray and I suspected that someone was rustling our stud ewes. The other man had been a stockman here until we fired him for drunkenness. He vowed to get even but we thought it was just an empty threat. Then when the sheep started disappearing, we put two and two together.'

'So you used the visit to the experimental paddock as an excuse to . . . what's the expression . . . stake the place out?' she queried.

'I won't ask where you learned expressions like that,' he said teasingly. 'But that's what we did. We moved in at dawn and caught them red-handed. Apparently, they'd had a heavy night drinking, so it wasn't too difficult to subdue them.'

'What will happen to them now?'

'The police are taking care of them and will probably want to interview you later on. Ray and I were in two-way radio contact with the local sergeant, so he was able to move in quickly once we located the camp.'

Lee could imagine Steve's terror when Tagg confronted him at the camp. He was very good at terrorising helpless women, but it was a different story when he was the one threatened, she had discovered. Like most bullies, he was a coward at heart. It was too bad she had taken so long to find it out. 'How did you know I had been there?' she asked, remembering.

Tagg's expression hardened. 'I searched the camp. When I went into his tent and found your hat on the floor, I added it up. Perry explained the rest, with a little more persuasion from me. He was lucky I didn't tear him apart. I certainly felt like it when I found out how he'd treated you.'

'How could you ever think I wanted to be there?' she asked, grimacing.

He looked uncomfortable. 'You must see how it looked to me. First, Steve Perry extorts money from Ray, and when I want to prosecute him you rush to his defence. That's when I started to worry about where your loyalties really lay.'

She ducked her head, shielding her shamed expression from him. 'Steve had threatened to tell everyone about my past if I didn't go along with him,' she confessed. 'I was afraid he would do it if I let you prosecute him.'

'I understand that now, but I didn't then. But you must have heard about sticks and stones . . .'

'This was more than words,' she said in a barely audible voice. She went on to tell him about Steve's attempt to force her to steal for him. 'I was so afraid of losing your love if you knew,' she finished.

He took her in his arms. 'Oh, Lee, as if anything could make me love you less! It tore me apart to leave you alone in that hotel, but when Perry arrived and announced he'd been there before me, I was afraid if I stayed I would do something I'd regret.'

'It wasn't what you thought,' she said urgently. 'The hotel told me my husband was waiting for me but when I rushed up to my room, he was there.'

'Were you really so eager to see me?' Tagg asked.

'I practically flew up to my room! When I saw who it was, I threw him out on his ear. I told him if he ever came near me again I'd let you prosecute him and give evidence myself, no matter what he did to me.'

Tagg chuckled. 'The worm really did turn!'

'Funny, that's what he said. I suppose it's true. I know when I found him there instead of you, I decided I didn't care what happened to me as long as you knew the truth.'

'And now I do,' Tagg said huskily. 'I promise I'll never doubt you again, my love. Half my problem is that I was insanely jealous of Steve Perry for having first claim on you.'

'But yours is the last and most important claim,' she said decisively. 'Don't ever forget that.'

'Speaking of forgetting, I was supposed to tell you

that Karen is bringing Cheryl back to Mundoo today. It seems she's made such spectacular progress that her doctor decided to let her come home and spend the rest of her pregnancy here. I've sent Ray back to tell everyone I found you and you're all right. They'll be waiting for us when we get back.'

Lee looked at him through lowered lashes. 'Do you suppose they could wait a little longer?'

His gaze grew hot and he tilted her back so she was cradled in the crook of his arm. 'Maybe a lot longer.'

Her heart started to race again, but this time with anticipation, instead of fear. He buried his head in the cleft between her breasts and she clasped her arm around him, drawing him closer. How could she ever have dreaded his embraces? Now she craved them, and she let him know with every subtle movement of her body and each murmur of her lips against his.

'Happy, darling?' he asked her.

She gathered his full upper lip between her teeth, nibbling daintily before she answered, 'What do you think?'

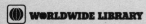

Harlequin Intrigue
Adopts a New Cover Story!

We are proud to present to you the new Harlequin Intrigue cover design.

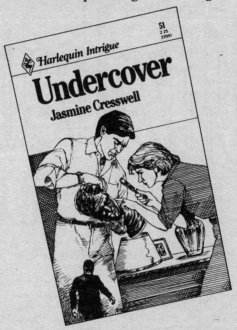

Look for two exciting new stories each month, which mix a contemporary, sophisticated romance with the surprising twists and turns of a puzzler . . . romance with "something more."

CAROLE MORTIMER

JUST ONE NIGHT

Hawk Sinclair—Texas millionaire and owner of the exclusive
Sinclair hotels, determined to protect his son's inheritance.
Leonie Spencer—desperate to protect her sister's happiness.

They were together for just one night.
The night their daughter was conceived.

Blackmail, kidnapping and attempted murder add suspense
to passion in this exciting bestseller.

The success story of Carole Mortimer continues with *Just
One Night*, a captivating romance from the author of the
bestselling novels, *Gypsy* and *Merlyn's Magic*.

**Available in March
wherever paperbacks are sold.**